FALLING FOR THE OMEGA

HOBSON HILLS: BOOK ONE

C.W. GRAY

Carter loaded the last of his tools into his new work van and shut the door. His first day in his new profession was off to a good start. He had three clients to see today and eight spread out during the rest of the week.

Finally getting his plumbing license had been a good idea, even if his perfect, wealthy family hated the idea of him being a plumber.

Hell, they had also hated the idea of him being a soldier and of him moving out of state when he came back injured. They pretty much hated every decision he made.

The crisp fall wind was cold, but the gold, brown, and red leaves on the trees and ground made the cold worth dealing with. Autumn in Maine sure wasn't the same as autumn in Georgia, but so far, he was damn happy with the move. There was a peace here amongst the trees that he hadn't managed to find anywhere else.

"Hi, Mr. Neighbor!"

A child's voice came from behind him, startling Carter. He spun around, stumbling a bit on his prosthesis, and faced the little girl standing a few feet from his van.

She looked about five or six, with two black braids, caramel skin, and a freckled nose. When she smiled brightly, he saw a small gap between her two front teeth.

A black and gray miniature schnauzer sat at her feet, gaze stern and trained on him.

He looked around and didn't see any adults. His little half acre tract was quite a ways back from the road, nestled between a good-sized apple orchard on one side and a thick forest on the other.

Where the hell had this little girl come from?

"My name's Olive, and I brought you a welcome basket. I made it myself, but Daddy made you one too. He's gonna bring it tonight. I wanted you to get mine first, 'cause it's from me and then we'll be best friends." The little girl paused to take a breath. Her wide brown eyes sparkled and met his straight on, innocent and fearless. "We'll be best friends forever."

She didn't even seem to see the scars along the side of his face. The burn marks had already made two kids cry at the grocery store yesterday. Both times, the parents had been too embarrassed to apologize. They just grabbed their kids and ran.

"Uh, where's your daddy, Olive?" His voice was deep and cracked, broken by the scarring on his neck. Her adoring stare was starting to freak him out a little. He'd never really been around kids.

"He's at home," she answered and handed him the basket. "See what I brought you? Look, look, look."

"Do you know your phone number? Maybe we could give your daddy a call," Carter said, taking the basket from Olive. He pulled the small hand towel from the top and almost dropped the basket. "Is that a hedgehog?"

"Yep! That's Hodges the hedgehog. He wanted to come visit too. Oh and this is Winston," she said and knelt to pet the small dog.

"Okay, your number?" He tried to keep his gruff voice kind. No sense in scaring the kid.

"Olive! Olive Persephone Wilson! Where are you?" A man's voice called from the orchard, full of panic and desperation.

"Uh oh," Olive said. She hurriedly looked around, then darted behind his van, Winston following her. "That's Daddy." She poked her head out and stared hard. "Tell. Him. Nothing."

She quickly hid again when a young omega rushed out of the orchard. He was her father, had to be. He looked just like her.

Carter suddenly couldn't catch his breath. The man in front of him was simply adorable. He was short and well formed, a little chubby. His black hair fell in curls around his face, and his wide hazel eyes contrasted beautifully with his caramel skin. The same freckles that decorated his daughter's nose, fell across his own. Where it looked cute on the kid, on her father... Bad thoughts, Carter! Bad thoughts!

"Have you seen a little girl? Black hair? Brown eyes?

Miniature schnauzer with her? Maybe a hedgehog?"

Carter stared at the handsome man, mouth gaping, for too long.

The man frowned at him, tilting his head. "Are you alright?" His shy smile revealed the small gap between his front teeth.

Oh fuck, he was so damn perfect. He met Carter's eyes too, didn't even glance at the scars.

"Mister?"

Carter shook his head and did his best to pull himself together. He smiled, as best he could with the scar tissue, and nodded toward the van, holding a finger to his lips, encouraging the man to keep quiet.

Olive's father rolled his eyes and stomped around the van. A squealing Olive ran from her hiding spot and hid behind Carter, hugging him around the waist.

"Mr. Neighbor, save me!" Her giggling told him she wasn't too worried about her father catching her.

"Olive, you scared me to death running off like that." Her father really did look worried. "What have I told you about leaving the house without me?"

"But daddy," she whined. "I wanted to meet Mr. Neighbor. We're best friends now, and I gave him a welcome basket. I was being hospital."

Carter frowned. Hospital?

"Hospitable, baby girl, and it doesn't matter. You are too little to be wandering around by yourself and talking to strangers. No television time this week, and you have to clean out Pooka and Banjo's stalls on Saturday."

Olive gave a big sigh and leaned her forehead into

Carter's leg. "Okay, Daddy, but it was worth it. I have a new best friend now."

The man met Carter's stare, a question in his eyes. Carter nodded and gave his best half smile.

"Well, maybe our new neighbor would like to come over for dinner one night? So that we can meet him properly," the man said.

"Yay! Mr. Neighbor, can you come tonight? Daddy's gonna make apple dumplins for dessert."

Carter smiled at the little girl and nodded. "Yeah, if it's okay with your dad."

The man smiled and nodded eagerly. "That would be great. I hardly ever get to cook for anyone but Olive." He gave a flustered look and held out his hand. "Oh, I forgot. My name is Elijah Wilson. I live in the farmhouse with the orchard. Of course, you've met Olive."

Carter shook his hand, touch lingering longer than it should. He was reluctant to release him but finally did. "Yeah, I'm Carter Benson. Just moved here from Georgia."

"Wow, so Maine's probably a bit different, huh?"

"Yeah, but all the colors on the trees? And ya'll actually have snow. I've never seen much of it."

"You say that like snow is a good thing." Elijah shuddered. "Well, welcome to Hobson Hill. I see Olive already gave you a welcome basket."

Carter looked back in it. "There's a hedgehog in there." His coarse voice was getting rougher as he spoke. He wasn't used to talking so much. Doctors said it was good for him to do though.

"I put cider in there for you. It's in my favorite big girl cup, the one with Moana. There's also butter from Pooka and some of Daddy's bread. It's so yummy!"

"Thanks, Olive. I appreciate it," Carter said. The little girl still hung on his leg, smiling up at him. She was a cute one, he acknowledged, even though she was clearly a little crazy. It was a good crazy though.

"Your alpha won't mind me coming," Carter asked Elijah.

The man winced and lowered his eyes. "I don't have an Alpha, so no, that won't be a problem."

Carter was surprised. Happy, but surprised. This adorable man had to be beating them off with a stick. Of course, some folks thought poorly about single omegas, and some alphas refused to even speak to them. Idiots.

"I guess I'll see you tonight. What time?"

"Oh, is six okay?" Elijah's confidence seemed to bounce back at Carter's question.

"That's fine. I better get to work."

"Yes, of course," Elijah said and pulled Olive off Carter's leg. "Come on, Olive. We better get back to the house. We need to get you to school."

"Okay. Bye, Carter, love you!" The little girl and her dog ran off through the orchard.

"I swear it's exhausting keeping up with her," Elijah sighed. Carter smiled and held the hedgehog out to him. "Thanks," he said, taking Hodges and smiling shyly. "See you tonight. Have a good day at work."

Carter stood frozen as he watched Elijah walk away. He was in trouble. Big, wonderful trouble.

CHAPTER 2

Once Olive was safely on the school bus, Elijah let himself freak out. His new neighbor was damn intriguing, and he seemed to like Olive and Elijah both. He did a little dance in the driveway, shaking his butt. He stopped and quickly looked around. Luckily, living in the middle of an apple orchard kept the prying eyes to a minimum. So he danced.

He danced all the way into the house, stopping on the porch to stroke Boo's back as the lazy black cat lounged in a chair. Then he danced all the way to the barn and quickly milked Pooka, his jersey cow. He fed her some treats and rubbed her silky nose. Then he danced while he tossed some fresh hay into Banjo's hay rack, watching the miniature donkey munch his breakfast.

By the time he danced back to the house, he was a little tired. He plopped onto the couch and dialed his best friend.

"Elijah, how goes it?" Zoe's voice was sassy, just like her. His cousin looked just like him, except for her coloring, but she had gotten all the confidence and charisma.

"I'm in love!"

"Wow, okay, this is unexpected, but, Elijah, I'm just not that into you, and we *are* cousins."

"Eww, that's so gross. No, no, no."

Zoe laughed, snorting a little. "So who is it? Is it Tanner Jones? I know he's been asking you out for a while, but he was a jerk to you in school, so I'm not sure it's a good idea."

"He's really gotten a lot nicer, but no, it's not Tanner. Now stop guessing, you're horrible at it. So, I guess I'm not really in love, but I am seriously in lust with my new neighbor."

"The guy Gramps was talking about? The soldier?"

"Yes," Elijah replied. "I met him today, and he is so sweet. He likes Olive too."

"Well, Gramps did the background check when he rented him the trailer, so I guess he isn't likely to be a serial killer." She hummed for a minute. "Or maybe he's a really good serial killer."

"No, Zozo, he is perfect, not a serial killer. He's so tall and muscled. Yummy!"

"Seriously, Elijah, you never talk like this. You really like this guy? You haven't dated anyone since he-who-must-not-be-named in college. Honestly, I wouldn't really call that dating, more like secretly hooking up."

"I haven't had time, Zoe. You know that, and really, who would date me right after I had Olive? Most of the town hated me, the ones not related to me anyway. Hell, at least a quarter of the town still hates me, because I'm a single parent and an omega."

"Gramps and Grammy nipped that shit in the bud when you came home. You've gotten lots of interest from alphas in town recently. What's so special about this one? What has you finally coming out of your shell?"

"I don't know," he admitted. "I just know that he's different, special. It's like I'm on the verge of something wonderful. I just have to take the first step."

"Aww, Eli, that's great. When do I get to meet him?"

"Hold on now, I need to actually go out with him before I submit him to you or the rest of the family. I don't want to scare him off, and Olive already started that process this morning by claiming him as her *best friend forever*."

"I love that girl," Zoe said with a happy sigh. The two were like two peas in a pod. It wasn't a good thing. "Crap, I gotta go. Sylvie and Jonny are getting slammed up front. I'll call you tonight, okay?" Zoe owned a bakery in town, and it stayed pretty busy from open to close.

"After ten. He's coming over for dinner at six."

"Oh my God, your first date," she squealed. "Next, it'll be your Star Wars themed wedding, just like you planned when you were twelve. Oh my God, I don't have a Princess Leia dress."

Elijah hung up on the crazy woman before she burst his eardrum. Anyway, she was wrong. He'd be

Princess Leia, not her, because it would be *his* wedding. Ridiculous.

He jumped up, eager to go. He needed to get to work while he had the time. He technically had three jobs. He made enough money to pay the day-to-day bills as an online adjunct instructor for business and accounting classes at a local community college and a nearby private university.

It wasn't much pay, but he owned the house and orchard, and Olive and him weren't big spenders. He taught a total of five online classes per semester and that took a good chunk of his time.

His second job was to help out with his grandparent's farm. They owned a lot of property, but their kids and grandkids were the ones who worked the land, making their own living. Every Wilson received a portion of the farm's earnings, and Elijah always made sure that he really *earned* it.

His main contribution was the apple orchard. In the fall, he made the apple cider, apple bread, and apple butter that sold so well in their little store down the road. He also helped Grammy with her passion: cranberries. The woman was seventy-two, but loved working her damn cranberry farm. Elijah had to admit, though, he enjoyed helping her.

His grandparents and extended family made a good living, despite *just being farmers*, as his parents put it. His Uncle Barry was a party planner and rented out two separate barns on the property for weddings and events. Uncle Marco used their pasture for a large number of cattle. He had a contract with the local stores that brought in a lot of money.

His Aunt Anna managed the store, though his grandparents often came in to socialize and help out. The tourists flocked there in droves, even in the winter. They sold products produced by the family, from his grandparents to several cousins. All year round, they sold fresh eggs and milk, homemade butter, yarn made from his cousin Ernie's alpaca and sheep herds, and another cousin's handmade furniture and knickknacks.

In the spring, they sold his cousin Janelle's flowers and fresh maple syrup collected and made by Elijah from trees all over the property. In the summer, they sold fresh fruits and vegetables and canned goods. In the fall, the store sold his apple products, Grammy's cranberries, pumpkins and gourds, and a variety of nuts. In the winter, they opened up the Christmas tree farm and held community events at the small, frozen pond near the store. All in all, the family did well with the farm, and it sure provided for them.

His third job was a secret between him and Gramps. It was to make sure the farm kept providing for each family member. Every Wilson had a stake in the farm, an investment, and his grandparents wanted to make sure their kids and grandkids benefitted from all their hard work.

When he was born, Gramps started the Wilson Education Fund to pay for college for his future grandkids. When Aunt Anna had her first miscarriage and the medical bills started piling up, Gramps started the Wilson Emergency Fund.

Now, it was Elijah's job to manage them, as well as invest for the future. He may not be a CEO of a big company, but he sure put his MBA and investing talents to work.

Elijah gathered up the newest batch of apple bread and apple butter and loaded it into his Jeep. Winston jumped into the passenger seat, and Elijah fastened his dog seatbelt. Then they were off, driving down the winding road to the store.

Autumn in Maine was a beautiful sight, and he could understand Carter's enjoyment of the colors, scents, and smells. He personally loved sweater weather, but he did dread the cold of winter.

The road wound through the forest and pastures, all owned by his grandparents. His aunt and uncles had houses on the property and several of his cousins chose to live there too, their own homes dotted across the landscape.

Grammy loved having her family so close, but Gramps often joked about wanting some peace and quiet. He sure spent a lot of time with his grandkids though.

A short, two-minute drive brought him to Farm Fresh. There was already a crowd milling about the store, so Elijah pulled around back to unload. He let Winston out and opened the back of the Jeep. Allison, one of his youngest cousins, came out and started helping him.

"They are going crazy for the apple bread today.

Mama said to get your butt up top and start baking some more."

"This isn't enough?" He'd baked over a hundred loaves that morning.

"She wants more and says the smell of it baking makes it sell even faster."

"You're supposed to be at school. Why are you hanging out here?"

"I'm riding in with Milly after I help you unload." She grinned, a classic Wilson smile with the small gap in her front teeth.

"Thanks, Allison, but I got this. Get to school. Your freshman year in high school only happens once."

"Thank God it only happens once." She laughed and grabbed her backpack from beside the door. "See you later, cousin."

Elijah set the first box of bread down on the counter, then quickly got the other boxes. Aunt Anna was already unloading his goods and bringing the bread up front.

"Bake me some bread, boy," she yelled, laughing. She gave him a big sloppy kiss on his cheek as he passed her.

"Yes, ma'am, but I have to leave by twelve to help Grammy with the cranberries."

"You're such a good boy, Eli-baby," she said, smiling softly at him. "I'll keep track of the time for you."

Elijah climbed the curving, wrought iron steps leading to the small kitchen in the loft. The family kept a lot of supplies there just in case more baking or canning was needed in a pinch. Sure enough, a box of apples sat on a counter, waiting on him to get started.

As he worked, the smell of fresh baked bread filled the store, and he knew his bread would be sold out by that afternoon.

He wondered if Carter liked bread. Olive had given him some in her basket, and the idea of the handsome man eating something Elijah made with his own hands was intoxicating. He'd make him a good meal tonight, show him he could take care of him.

Elijah shook his head. Damn omega genes were getting carried away. Next, he'd be thinking babies. Hmm, Carter's babies would be so cute. They'd be little chubby cuties with his reddish brown hair and soulful brown eyes. "Double damn it," he said.

"What's bothering you, Eli-baby?" Anna finished climbing the stairs and went to the coffee pot, pouring herself a cup.

His aunt was a beautiful woman. She was tiny, blond, and feisty as hell. He absolutely adored her.

"Nothing, Auntie," he said quickly. He didn't need his family figuring out his crush. He shouldn't have told Zoe, but he was so excited.

"Hmm, that just makes me sure there's something," she said, voice rich and deep. He remembered that melodious voice singing him lullabies as a kid, holding him close and rocking him.

"Okay, okay," he said, giving in easily. One more person knowing wouldn't hurt, right? He'd just give her a hint, enough to pacify her. "I met an alpha today, and I want to climb him like White Cap Mountain."

That hadn't really come out the way he'd meant it to.

Her burst of laughter filled the air. "Oh my, Eli-baby," she said. "Who is he, and when do I get to meet him?"

"Why does everyone want to meet him? I want to actually date him before introducing him to the family."

"Date him? Oh my word, I am so happy to hear that. I thought you'd given up on alphas since he-who-must-not-be-named did a number on you. Who is he?"

"His name's Carter Benson, and Gramps rented the trailer next to the orchard to him. Olive provided a meet cute, a dangerous, panic-inducing meet cue, and he's coming by for dinner tonight."

"Oh good! I was hoping there'd be a new baby in the family soon. I'm so glad you're going to settle down and give Mom and Dad some more great-grand babies. Lord knows your cousins are taking their time." She clapped her hands and headed for the stairs.

"What?! I said he was coming for dinner. That's not how babies are made," Elijah said.

He aunt ignored him and hummed a happy song as she left.

"Triple damn it," he muttered.

CHAPTER 3

Carter lay under Mrs. Weber's kitchen sink, inspecting the leaky pipe. The middle-aged woman hadn't stopped chattering since he'd come in the door. She seemed nice enough, maybe just a little lonely.

"So, I heard you rented the trailer next to the apple orchard on the Wilson farm." She didn't wait for his response. "You need to watch out for your neighbor. Elijah Wilson is an omega whore. Doesn't know how to keep his legs closed and that little bastard of his is proof of it," she said, contempt dripping on every hateful word.

Carter closed his eyes tightly. He saw Olive standing in front of him with a welcome basket. He saw Elijah's shy smile as he invited him to dinner. He slid out from under the sink and grabbed his tools, packing them back up.

"You're finished already?" she asked in surprise. "I'd thought that'd take at least an hour."

"Call someone else," he said, voice rougher than usual. "I don't work for bigots."

"Bigot! I'm not a bigot," she said. "This about Elijah Wilson? That's what most everyone says about him in town. Well, everyone he's not related to." She was flustered, but stood in her doorway, blocking him from leaving. "I'm not a bigot," she said, nodding firmly.

"You just insulted a guy you clearly don't really know based on him being an omega and a single parent. That makes you a damn bigot," he said and growled. "Plus, you just called a sweet little five-year-old a bastard. How's that right?"

"But... he had her when was eighteen," she said softly. "He graduated high school at fifteen, and his grandparents sent him to college. He was in the last year of a MBA and got pregnant. Didn't know who to put on the birth certificate. A good moral boy wouldn't do that, omega or not."

"He was finishing college at eighteen, and you're saying he's some frivolous omega?" Carter said in disbelief. "You have teenagers of your own. You think they can even handle the social pressure of college right now, little less the brains side of it? You said your daughter's fifteen and your son's seventeen, right?"

She frowned. "Well, they're good kids, but Josh is still too immature, he'll grow up soon enough. I have to watch my Cassidy though. She's a people pleaser, a cute boy pays her a bit of attention and she'll do the stupidest things."

"So your daughter goes to college and gets

pregnant," he said. "You going to call her a whore that can't keep her legs closed?"

Mrs. Weber gasped, looking horrified. "Of course not! Kids make mistakes all the time, and parents need to be there to love and accept them... oh," she said, deflating and pale. "Oh."

"I'm going to fix your sink, ma'am," he said. "But don't call me again unless you can keep your insults to yourself."

He lay back down at the sink and quickly changed out the leaky joint, then turned the water back on. Mrs. Weber sat at the kitchen table, watching him solemnly.

His next client was another house wife, younger with three kids under five at home. Mrs. Roxwell didn't have time to breathe, much less gossip. Her youngest, a two-year-old, sat on the basement floor, sucking his thumb, and watched Carter the whole time. His mother was glad for the break from her most rumbustious kid and left him in Carter's care. He shrugged and installed the new water heater fairly quickly. At the door, the little boy waved goodbye from behind his mother's legs. Maybe he wasn't so bad with kids. At least, he hadn't made any cry that day.

His last client of the day met him at the door in a boldly patterned silk romper, high heels, and a full face of makeup. Mr. Bartley was Carter's new favorite person. He was unapologetically male, but loved feminine clothing. He was a beta and a retired pilot.

"So, you live out on the Wilson farm now, hmm?" he said, handing Carter a mug of coffee as he contemplated the man's corroded bathroom pipes. Carter looked at him warily and sipped his coffee.

"What about it?" he asked.

"Well, Mr. Grumpy," the older man said, "I'm going to give you a warning."

Carter didn't like the sound of this. He didn't want to yell at his new favorite person.

"You be extra fucking nice to your neighbor and his daughter. They are both sweethearts who get enough shit from some of the snotty-ass people in this town. They don't need it from you too."

Carter couldn't stop his half grin. He knew he liked this man.

"Oh fuck, that smile," Mr. Bartley said. "It's so ugly, but so beautiful. Ugh." He threw up his hands and strode out of the guest bathroom.

Carter's smile stayed in place as he wrote up an estimate on the replacement of the pipes, giving the man a hefty discount.

"Next week, on Wednesday," Mr. Bartley agreed. "Now hurry up and go. I've got a special friend coming over, and I need to make myself beautiful." He pressed a to-go cup of hot coffee into Carter's hands and pushed him out the door.

It was only a little after one when he finished for the day, and Carter was hungry. His delicious apple bread and cider had disappeared quickly between his first two jobs. He tried not to think too hard on how pleased he'd been to eat something Elijah made.

He walked along the picturesque streets of Hobson Hill, admiring the fall decorations. The weather was cool, and he pulled his thin coat close, knowing he'd have to get a thicker one soon. Georgia was worlds away from New England. The town looked like something out of a Hallmark movie. Each store and house was decorated with pumpkins, squash, corn stalks, and fall flowers.

It all came together to present the image of the perfect town. Then Carter remembered Mrs. Weber's words from earlier. It was far from a perfect town if that's how people saw Elijah. He thought of Mr. Bartley and decided there were some redeeming factors.

He came across a little café called Cozy Kitchen and decided to give it a try. It was next to a bakery called Honey Buns that Carter might try out in the morning. The door rang as he walked in, and the whole room turned to look at him. Maybe this wasn't a good idea. He had almost forgotten about his face.

"Hey there," the perky blond omega behind the bar said. "Have a seat wherever you like. Menus are on the table."

Carter nodded in thanks and shuffled to an empty table against a window in the far back. He looked the menu over and almost jumped out of his seat when the omega suddenly appeared at his table.

"Hi, what can I get you to drink?"

"Water, please," Carter said softly. His voice was starting to go, and he needed to rest it a bit.

"Perfect! By the way, my name is Abel. You're new to town, right?"

"Yeah. Name's Carter Benson."

"Carter Benson," Abel repeated with a squeak. He

grinned and Carter was surprised to see a familiar gap between his two front teeth. He didn't share Elijah's coloring, but he judged their features were similar enough now that he was looking for it.

"Oh, oh, oh," he said, hopping in place. "I'll, uh, go get your water." He was pulling his phone from his pocket before he even made it to the kitchen.

Well that was strange, Carter thought. He looked back at the menu and decided on a haddock sandwich. He couldn't wait until he got to see Elijah again. Carter couldn't remember ever being so excited about a date before. Of course, this wasn't a date. It was a friendly dinner with a new neighbor. He needed to keep that in mind before he did something stupid.

There was no way in hell that a wonderful omega like Elijah would go for a broken man like Carter. He had a trust fund, but that was about the only thing he had going for him. The sweet man and his little girl could do far better.

"Here's your water, sir," a young woman said. She must have noticed his puzzled look. "Sorry, but Abel's taking his break, and I'll be serving you today." She smiled, friendly as could be. "What can I get you?"

Carter had just finished ordering when Abel and two strangers ran up and sat at his table.

"So, guys this is Elijah's Carter," Abel said, gesturing grandly toward Carter. "Carter, this is Zoe and Ernie, my brother and sister. We're Elijah's cousins."

The woman smiled widely, eyeing him like a piece of meat. "Elijah wasn't lying when he said you were hot."

"What?" Elijah thought he was hot? A slow grin crept across his face. But… his scars? He gestured to his face. "With these?"

The woman looked a lot more like Elijah than Abel, but her coloring was similar to her brother's. She was blond, with bronze skin, and brown eyes.

"Oh, sweetie, those scars are nothing. Just a little part of your handsomeness," she replied. Her words gave him pause. Is that how Elijah saw his scars? Just a small part of him?

"Geez, Zoe, stop eying the man like he's dinner," the other man, Ernie, said. "So, tell us all about yourself." Ernie leaned forward, eyes wide and focused. "Tell us everything."

At that point, Carter's voice was too hoarse to be very coherent, but he tried. "What do you want to know?"

"Oh dear, is your throat hurting?" Abel asked. When Carter nodded, he glared at his sister and brother. "No interrogations today. He needs to save his voice for tonight."

Zoe smiled an evil smile. "We'll just tell you about Elijah. Would you like to hear some stories about when he was a kid? He's the oldest of all us cousins, but only by a year or two. We know all the good stuff."

Carter grinned and nodded. He wanted to know everything about his omega. Damn it, not *his* omega. Elijah, just Elijah. He happily settled into the booth to listen to the cousins' stories.

"Okay, so when he was eight," Ernie began, "he decided he wanted to be a popstar."

CHAPTER 4

*E*lijah danced to the music on his phone's portable stereo as he pulled the pot roast out of the oven. He had been running a little behind due to grading, but things were back on track. His apple dumplings were in the second oven, ten more minutes to go, and the homemade yeast rolls were ready to bake. He popped them in the oven, shaking his butt.

"Daddy, Carter's here now, so stop being weird."

Elijah froze, turning around slowly. Sure enough, Olive stood in the kitchen doorway with Carter. His man was wet from the autumn rain, but he looked so damn good. He wore his gorgeous half smile, and his eyes were gleaming with laughter, even if he held it in.

"I'm gonna show him my room, 'kay?" Olive grabbed Carter's hand and pulled him up the stairs. "Come on so Daddy can dance some more. He does it all the time, but we gotta still love him. He's family."

Oh god, he thought, *please kill me now.*

Elijah shook it off. It hadn't happen, it hadn't happened. Now, time to mash those potatoes. He got to work, putting the finishing touches to dinner and setting the table.

He quietly climbed the stairs and tiptoed to Olive's room, peeking his head in. Winston lay on Olive's bed, watching as she sat in her window seat with Carter, showing him her books. Hodges sat in his little house, just now waking up.

"This is my favorite," she said, holding up *Harry Potter and the Sorcerer's Stone*. "Daddy said I can read the rest of the series when I get older, but I'm a big girl. Ms. Williams, my teacher, says I read like a fifth grader, but I'm just in first grade."

"That's great, Olive! I bet you're real smart, just like your daddy."

"Daddy says I am, but I hate math. He's real good at it, but it's icky."

Carter snorted. "I never liked it either. You can learn it though, you just have to keep trying." His deep voice was a little rough, but the smokiness was so damn sexy.

"Yeah, Daddy says it's a skill, not a gift," she said, then stuck her tongue out. "I still hate it."

"Well, tell me about this book. I watched the movie, I think. Why's it your favorite?"

Olive gave him a long, serious look. "I'm gonna tell you a secret. I didn't even tell Shelly, and she's my bestest friend."

"I thought I was your best friend," Carter said, amused.

"You're my best old person friend. Shelly is my best normal person friend."

Carter laughed. "Okay."

"So, I like this book anyways because it's awesome, but I heard Daddy and Zoe talking a few months ago…" She paused and looked at Carter, tilting her head. "You know how babies come, right?"

Carter blanched. "Uh…"

"Okay, I'll tell you. So when it's with an omega, like Daddy, the alpha and omega go to the bedroom and dance. Then, a long time later, Santa visits and helps the baby out of the omega's tummy."

"Okay," Carter said slowly. "You're sure it's Santa and not a doctor? What if the baby's born in summer or spring?"

"Of course it's Santa," she said, exasperated. "Santa does what Santa wants. He doesn't have to wait 'til Christmas."

"You're right. That makes sense."

"So, anyway, I heard Daddy and Zoe talking, and the alpha that Daddy danced with was Lord Voldemort." She sighed. "I'm Lord Voldemort's daughter."

Elijah's hung his head. Oh damn, he really needed to quit calling the asshole he-who-shall-not-be-named. And… he really needed to talk to Olive about where babies came from.

"Okay," Carter said calmly. "You sure? What'd you hear, exactly?"

"Zoe said that *he-who-shall-not-be-named* was a big meanie, and she didn't know how a good little girl like me could be from him." So, she paraphrased, but Elijah did remember that conversation.

"Oh, I see why you think it's Lord Voldemort," Carter said. "Your cousin Zoe just didn't want to say the alpha's name, so she used that phrase. Your alpha father's not Lord Voldemort."

"Really?" Olive sounded so relieved. "I don't want to be his daughter."

Oh Lord, his poor little baby girl. It was definitely time to tell her about the douchebag.

"I promise," Carter said, and Elijah walked into room, making sure they heard him approach.

"Hey guys," he said. "Ready for dinner?"

Carter looked up, relief in his eyes. "Oh yeah. Come on, Olive. Something smells really good."

The three settled in the kitchen. The large farmhouse had a dining room, but it was too big for just him and Olive. Usually, they ate right there at the cozy breakfast nook nestled against the bay window.

"This house is gorgeous, Elijah," Carter said between his moans as he ate the pot roast.

"It was my grandparents' house for most of their marriage. This is where they raised their four kids. It has six bedrooms, a full dining room, and a cute little sunroom. It even has a basement, but it's creepy, so I don't go down there. I did add solar panels to the back half of the roof and out at the barn, and I try to keep it maintained like they would have."

"It's a lot of space," Carter said. "It suits you though. Everything's warm and homey. I'm surprised your grandparents left."

Elijah smiled fondly. "About the time I had Olive, they decided they wanted to build a smaller house up the hill next to the cranberry bog. Grammy wanted less to keep up and to be closer to her berries. That woman is obsessed."

Carter laughed. "I bet you love helping her."

Elijah blushed. "Okay, so I do. I'm probably just as obsessed with my apples."

"He really is," Olive said. "Daddy, can we have apple dumplins now?"

"Of course."

After dinner, they watched Elijah and Olive's favorite movie, *Star Wars: The Force Awakens*. By the end of it, Olive was almost asleep.

"Time for your bath, baby girl."

Carter carried her upstairs, and Elijah ran her bath. They left her to it, returning to the living room.

Elijah sat on the couch in front of the stone fireplace and patted the seat beside him. "I won't bite," he said nervously. Damn but it had been a long time since he'd flirted with anyone. Carter sat close and laid his arm across the top. Elijah fit perfectly against his side.

"You have a nice home, Elijah. A nice family here."

"Thanks," he said softly. He loved Olive, but he was starting to think that he might actually want something more. "Are you settling into the trailer? It's small, but we've kept it up well."

"Yeah, it suits me," he said. "I didn't bring much with me when I joined the army and I've never been one to collect things."

"Gramps said you were in the army."

"I was." He was quiet for a moment, deep in thought. "A little over six months ago, we got ambushed, and I was one of the few to walk away from it. Left with these burns and missing half a leg, but I still lived."

"The other survivors? They alright?" Elijah had no idea how anyone could deal with a situation like that. The idea of his family or friends being hurt just about killed him.

"Yeah, for the most part. I stay in close contact with two of them. We've been friends since we enlisted."

Elijah snuggled into him, placing his head on Carter's chest. "I'm glad you're alive. I wish no one was hurt, but I'm glad you made it. I'm glad you've recovered so quickly."

"Me too," Carter said simply. "I got really lucky."

"I bet your family was happy you were alive," Elijah said.

"Yeah, I guess." Carter shrugged.

"You guess? What's that mean?"

"My family aren't bad people. They're actually really good people, but towards me, they're just a bit... critical. My parents come from wealthy, old money families and are very aware of their place in society. My dad's a lawyer, and my mom's all about her charities. My two brothers followed in Dad's footsteps. Both are lawyers in his law firm."

"Lawyers aren't *that* bad, right?" Elijah tried to mentally fit Carter in with the family he described.

"No," Carter said and laughed. "It's more that my parents have notions of what their kids should do and how they should behave. Those notions didn't include plumbing internships during the summer or joining the army after high school. They definitely didn't include actually becoming a plumber."

"Plumbers are really important," Elijah said, outraged on his behalf. "They're more important than stupid lawyers."

Carter started laughing, voice cracking. "Enough about them," he said. "So, I met some of your cousins today."

"Oh no," Elijah groaned. "Who was it, and what did they say?"

Carter laughed. "Zoe, Ernie, and Abel."

"That's Uncle Barry's bunch. Zoe is just a year younger than me, and she's my best friend, but it doesn't mean you can trust her. Don't believe anything they say."

"Your kitchen dancing has already proven at least three of their stories correct."

"I'm going to pretend that I didn't hear that and that you're still an innocent, having never met any of my family."

Carter chuckled and kissed the top of Elijah's head. "Does all of your family live here? It seems like there's a lot of them."

"Yeah, most of them, unless they're away at school. My parents and my younger brother are the only ones who don't."

"Where do they live?"

"Vegas last time I heard from them, but the last few cards I sent my brother were returned with 'wrong address,' and his phone's been disconnected, so I don't know."

"I take it you're not close to them?"

"I think I could be to my brother, but we've only met a couple times. We send each other holiday and birthday cards, but it's awkward talking to someone you don't really know but love anyway."

"Your parents? What about them?"

"My dad is the only one of Gramps and Grammy's four kids that doesn't live or work on the property. They both despise the whole state and very rarely visit. I don't think my grandparents would mind them not living here—they want their kids happy—but my mom and dad are both really nasty people. They're greedy, selfish, and judgmental."

"It must have been tough for you growing up with them." Carter hugged him close, wrapping both arms around Elijah.

"When I was born and they saw my omega line, they brought me to my grandparents, then ran away as fast as they could. They've only visited a handful of times. When I was older, I figured out they wanted an alpha son, not an omega. Not that I don't fully appreciate being raised by my grandparents. The only downside is not having a relationship with my brother."

"Damn, that sucks," Carter said. "I can't understand

how anyone wouldn't want to be around you. It's like you light up the world when you're here." He blushed and ducked his head.

Elijah smiled brightly, feeling lighter. "Thank you," he said. "You have no idea how much that means to me. This night's turning out pretty well, huh?

"Yeah," Carter said. "I'm here with you, not dead in the desert. You have Olive and the rest of your crazy family." He leaned in and gently kissed Elijah's lips, then pulled back.

"Carter, you can have me and Olive too, if you want us." Elijah had never felt so certain and so nervous at the same time.

Carter looked shocked. "You... You want me? I mean, for more than a kiss or a fuck?"

"Why the hell would I just want you for a kiss or a fuck?" What was wrong with his man? How could he not see his appeal?

"I'm broken, Elijah," Carter said. "I'm burned, I have a prosthesis, and sometimes I have really shitty dreams and wake up screaming. If I talk too much, my voice starts to go. Fuck, I'm a plumber. You could do so much better."

"You poor idiot," Elijah said sadly. "All that delusion. How do you get through the day? These scars and your leg? They're just part of you, and every single part of you is absolutely captivating. I knew you were beautiful when I saw you, and I can't wait to see what you're like on the inside." He stopped, tilting his head. "Wait, did that sound too serial killer like?"

Carter reluctantly smiled. "I think you may be the idiot, but I'll take you."

"Perfect," he said and leaned up to kiss him again.

The fire crackled and the rain started to pound against the tin roof. Perfect.

CHAPTER 5

The next month was honestly the best of Carter's life. With every second he spent with Elijah, he fell deeper and deeper in love with the omega. They had dinner every night and spent time talking and kissing after Olive went to bed. The more Carter learned about Elijah, the more he admired him.

A week ago, Elijah told him about he-who-shall-not-be-named and how his family really came together for him when Olive was born. Elijah had worked so damn hard to help his family and was there any time Olive needed him. He seemed to just smile and dance his way through everything.

Carter shook his head and grinned as he worked on the busted pipes in his client's bathroom. His omega was never far from his mind. He was so damn happy, and he wanted to tell someone, but who? He had become good friends with Ernie. The young omega was a third grade teacher and kept up an alpaca and sheep farm in his free time.

It seemed like every Wilson he met were hardworking overachievers. Ernie had even gifted him several knitted sweaters and scarfs. Carter seriously didn't know where the man found the time. Ernie already knew that Carter was crazy about his cousin though.

When Carter finished up, he headed into the cold rain. He went into Zoe's and shook like a dog, water shedding from his coat. Zoe didn't mind when he brought his lunch in instead of ordering her food.

Elijah had him good and spoiled. He packed him a lunch after dinner every night. Carter was a little afraid he would get fat from all the good food, but he couldn't make himself care all that much.

He waved at Zoe who glared at him, picking up the mop. He went to his usual table in the back and unpacked his homemade chicken salad sandwich, apple chips, and apple bread. He had been thinking hard about something but didn't know if he should do it or not. He didn't want to make Elijah mad.

"What are you thinking about so hard? You look like you need to poop." Zoe moaned as she sat, propping her feet up on a chair. She slid a hot cup of coffee across the table, fixed just the way he liked it. "The beard looks good though."

Since it was getting colder, Carter had grown a short beard. Elijah seemed to like it. He debated answering her question, but she may be the perfect person to ask. "I want to do something for Elijah, but I don't know if it would be too much."

"You should buy a princess-cut diamond, size eight, and propose at Sunday breakfast this week."

Carter shook his head. Zoe and Abel had started asking him when he planned to marry Elijah the day they met at the Cozy Kitchen. "I haven't been invited to Sunday breakfast yet," he said.

He wasn't worried about that. Not at all. Okay, maybe a little. Anyway, he had his great-grandmother's engagement ring, and he *may* have already had it sized. Maybe. Just in case.

Zoe snorted. "Oh, you have been invited, but the invitation hasn't made its way to you. Elijah wants to get you good and hooked before introducing you to the rest of the family. He doesn't want you running away, screaming in terror."

"I'm already good and hooked," he said roughly. "You could all be ghost clowns and I'd stay."

"Well then, you'd best show up to Grammy's by eight this Sunday." Zoe grinned and stole a chip. "If you're not proposing, what'd you want to do for our Elijah?"

"You know how he hasn't been able to get ahold of his brother?"

She sat up. "No. He never talks about his parents or Noah. What's going on?"

"He's sent him mail and tried to call, but can't reach him."

"That's weird. Noah has always kept in touch with him. Elijah won't say it, but he looks forward to the cards Noah sends."

"I thought I'd hire a private investigator to look into

it. See if I could find him. Elijah thinks he just doesn't want to talk to him anymore, like his parents, but I don't know. Do you think that would be too invasive?"

Zoe stood and kissed him on the head. "I think you are a sweet man, and you should break up with Elijah and marry me."

"So, it's a good idea then?" It sometimes seemed like Zoe spoke in riddles or something.

"Yep," she said and headed back to work. "It's a good idea."

Carter immediately texted his former army buddy, Raymond. He gave him Noah's full name and last known address. Raymond had started at a well-known security firm about a week ago, so he could probably handle the job.

Then he sent Raymond a picture Carter had taken last night, Elijah and him cuddled up on the couch, wrapped in a blanket. Carter was smiling his usual ugly smile, and Elijah was giving him a big kiss on the cheek.

After a minute, he sent the same picture to his oldest brother, Caden. Not that either Caden or Cain ever seemed to care about Carter, but it couldn't hurt. He waited a second, then sent it to his friend Juan too. Carter, Raymond, and Juan did their best to stay in touch since they were discharged, but it had been a while since he had texted or called them.

His phone rang. Carter grinned and answered without checking the screen. He'd known his buddies would want to know what was going on.

"Yeah?"

"Carter." Caden's voice was as perfectly controlled and calm as ever. "How are you doing?"

"Caden. Hey, I didn't… I'm fine. How're things going with you all?"

"We are all doing well. We recently landed two new, large accounts and father was awarded the John H. Pickering Achievement Award."

"Good. That's good."

"Is your leg alright? Have you fully adjusted to the prosthesis?"

"Yeah. Sometimes I forget I'm wearing it."

"How is your business faring?"

"Actually, really good. I've stayed busy since the first day, and it hasn't slowed down a bit. I still have time to rest my leg between clients though."

"Excellent," Caden said. "From your picture, I assume you met someone?"

Carter grinned and sighed happily. "Oh yeah. His name's Elijah, and he's the best damn thing to ever happen to me."

Carter forgot that he was talking to his brother. Forgot that he should be self-conscious. Forgot that Caden shouldn't give a damn about anything to do with him. He blathered on about Elijah for a good twenty minutes.

"I swear, Olive is the smartest little thing you'll ever meet. We're working our way through the third Harry Potter book now that Elijah's finally given her permission to read them."

"That series is advanced for a first grader. You enjoy reading with her?"

"Yeah, she's a sweet kid."

"Everything sounds... Wait a second... I need to let you go, Carter," Caden said. "Thank you for texting." He was quiet a second, and Carter almost hung up, thinking the call had ended. "Thank you," Caden said again. "Please... do not hesitate to call us for anything. Anything you need. You can call any of us. Goodbye, Carter."

Carter hung up, completely baffled. He had rarely had a full conversation with his older brothers about anything that didn't involve law, society parties, or his parents' expectations for Carter. He'd have to think on this.

He looked at his phone and noticed his buddies had called while he talked to Caden. He grinned and dialed them back, eager to talk some more about Elijah.

After lunch, Carter headed toward his last client for the day, the veterinarian clinic across town. The elderly vet had a busted pipe in the boarding room sink. Carter finished it quickly and was about to head up front for his payment when he heard the most pitiful, soulful whimpers.

He followed the sounds back to one of the occupied kennels. Inside was a white and grey ball of fur. As he approached, the puppy stopped whining and eagerly pressed against the door, tail wagging.

"Hey there, little guy," Carter said softly and knelt to pet the puppy through the wire.

"I see you found our little visitor," Duncan Grover said from the door. The older man stood just inside the room, carrying an unhappy cat. This was Carter's second visit to the vet, and he had quickly figured out that Dr. Grover was a good man that loved each and every one of his charges.

"He's adorable," Carter said, petting the puppy a little longer. Dr. Grover gently placed the cat into one of the open kennels, giving her a pat before shutting the cage.

"He is a cute one, an Old English Sheepdog. A man brought him in when he found him down by the lakeshore. He was malnourished and a mess. We cleaned him up, gave him his shots and some good meals. Now, he's as good as new. Tomorrow, I'm taking him to the animal shelter. They'll try to find him a home, I guess." The man sighed deeply and stared at Carter with sad, sad eyes. "If only we could find him a forever home before he had to become just one puppy among many."

"You're a horrible man," Carter said, opening the puppy's door and taking him out. "Is he my payment?"

Dr. Grover laughed and followed him to the front. "I'll still pay you, but I will waive the adoption fee. I knew Elijah's boyfriend couldn't possibly resist a cute little puppy."

Carter smiled, pleased that the news of them being a couple had spread around town.

Dr. Grover smiled. "Tomorrow, I'm going out to his house to try to convince him to take a goat some farmer left at our back fence. I swear, people can be annoying."

"I'll go ahead and take the goat too, if I can

transport him in the back of my van. You know Elijah will take him."

Dr. Grover nodded and smiled widely. "He's a baby, so I have a carrier he can fit in right here. It's a short drive, so it shouldn't be a problem. I know you'll be back soon enough with this old building's bad plumbing. You can return it then."

"You weren't going to bring him the goat, were you?" Carter eyed the veterinarian.

Dr. Grover winked and chuckled, then went to get the carriers for the goat and puppy. He packed him a box of supplies and sent Carter on his way.

Elijah was waiting for him on the old farmhouse's porch when Carter pulled into the drive. He got out, carrying Hotdog. Yes, he had already named the dog. He had always wanted a dog, but his parents hadn't wanted to bother with the mess. Hotdog would be his first pet.

"Who you got there?"

"This is Hotdog, my dog." Carter gave him a sheepish look. "Um, there's a baby goat for you in the back of the van."

"Yes, Dr. Grover gave me a call to tell me what to feed our new boy," he said, amusement filling his eyes. "He marked you for the softy you are. There's no telling how many pets we end up with now."

Carter shrugged and grinned. "You have a big place out here."

Elijah gave him a nervous look as he carried the goat to the barn, Carter and Hotdog following along. "That's something I wanted to talk to you about, but you've got to promise not to get mad or freak out, okay?"

Carter leaned down and kissed the top of his head. "I promise to do my best."

"Okay, so, you've been coming over every night for the last few weeks, and we've all been spending a lot of time together. Olive, you, and me."

"Yeah, is that okay? If you want me to back off, I can. I just really like spending time with the two of you."

"No! No backing off," he said loudly, startling Pooka and Banjo as they poked their heads over the stall to investigate. "It's the opposite, actually. I'd really like it if you moved your stuff over here."

"Really?" Carter was pleased, but a little confused. "We haven't even had sex yet. Not that I'm complaining. I've been enjoying our make-out sessions." He opened the stall Elijah gestured toward.

"Me too, and if you don't have to leave at night, we can spend more *quality* time together once Olive goes to sleep. Though, Zoe is watching Olive tomorrow night and Saturday. They needed some girl time. If you don't want to move in, we'll have more time then. I'm not trying to manipulate you with sex. We'll get there either way." Elijah set the baby goat down. "He'll be good here for now, but let's get him a stall ready next to Banjo."

The two men talked about their days as they cleaned out a stall and put hay down on the ground.

"My brother didn't complain about me being a plumber once. Not once!"

"That's awesome. Maybe your family's missing you and thinking about the consequences of their criticism."

"Maybe. I don't know. It was only one call."

"I'll work on fixing the stall up some more later," Elijah said. "Now, this little guy needs some milk."

Carter watched, strangely happy, as Elijah fed the little goat. "I'd love to move in, Elijah," he said. "I know it's only been a few weeks, but I love you and Olive. We can make it work."

Elijah's smile lit up the whole barn. "I can't believe you just told me you love me for the first time while I'm bottle feeding a goat."

"Timing's everything," he said with a grin. "Do you think Olive will be upset with me moving in?"

"Definitely not. I talked to her a couple nights ago about her father."

"Lord Voldemort?"

"Very funny, but yes, him." Elijah groaned and leaned back against the stall's wall. "How do you tell a five-year-old that her alpha father didn't want her? That he wanted to marry someone else and start a family without her?"

"Oh, damn," Carter said, sadness filling him. "Did it break her heart? She seemed fine last night."

"Well, she cried and asked some really fucking difficult questions," Elijah said. "Then the next morning, while we waited for the bus, she tells me that you're going to be her papa."

"She really said that?" Carter didn't think he could be any happier.

Elijah laughed. "Oh yeah. She said that you'd be her papa and that she *knew* you wanted to be her papa, because you loved her."

"Damn right I do!"

"That made me think, 'what the hell am I waiting for?' I knew I loved you, and you've been so good for her. If I was so certain, then why wait?"

Carter leaned over the goat and kissed his omega. "I'm going to go get my things right now. I can have everything unpacked before Olive gets home from school." He jumped up and ran to his van, limping a little. Stopped. Turned around and ran back. "I forgot Hotdog."

The puppy was sitting in a pile of hay at Elijah's feet. "I've got him, Softie McSoftster. Go get your stuff."

CHAPTER 6

Olive finally went to bed, after making Carter read her two bedtime stories and tuck her in. Elijah's daughter had been so damn happy that Carter was moved in. He knew that anytime now she'd call him papa, and Carter would be completely at her mercy. The little brat knew what she was doing.

Elijah finished brushing his teeth, rinsed his mouth, then went back into the bedroom. Carter sat on the bed, fully clothed, looking pretty damn nervous. "Carter, are you alright?"

His alpha looked at him, eyes vulnerable. "I forgot that if we share a room, you'd see all my scars and my leg."

Elijah made a choked sound. "So delusional…"

He pushed Carter's legs apart and stood between them. He started unbuttoning Carter's shirt, making quick work of it, and pushed it off his broad shoulders. The scars on his face continued down his neck and his left shoulder, stopping at his elbow. They were lighter on his neck and arm, less noticeable. His thick, well-muscled chest begged for Elijah's mouth.

He placed gentle kisses on the scars along Carter's face, kissing his neck, then making his way down the scarred shoulder and ending at his elbow. "I can't believe you think these scars make a difference to me. I see you, Carter. I see *you*."

His mouth finally got what it wanted: Carter's nipple. His teeth pulled at the little peaked nub, drawing a groan from his alpha. Meanwhile, his hands worked on Carter's belt, his alpha panting heavily.

Carter lay back on the bed, soft eyes watching closely as Elijah pulled his pants down his legs. He had already removed his prosthesis, so his stump was visible as his pants hit the floor. Elijah ran his hands along Carter's legs, one on each.

"You're my alpha, Carter. All of you. Your scars, your prosthesis, your broad shoulders, firm ass, all of it. All mine."

"Yes," Carter whispered. "All yours."

Elijah pulled his pajama top off, revealing his slim shoulders, well-padded hips, and soft belly. Carter's intense brown eyes were locked on his every movement.

Elijah felt an insane amount of power as he slid his pajama pants off, leaving his wool socks on. His feet got cold, damn it. They were extremely sexy if Carter's molten gaze was any indication.

Elijah knelt at the end of the bed, between Carter's

legs. His mouth slowly moved up his alpha's body, leaving kisses and licks along the way. His tongue darted out, licking behind Carter's knee, and he jumped, his dick tenting his boxers.

Finally, Elijah's eyes settled on Carter's lap. He slowly peeled the boxers down, then took his alpha in his mouth, closing around him and sucking. He was too big to fit completely, but damn, he tasted so hot and sweet.

It wasn't long before Carter was bucking his hips and gripping his hair. "Wanna come in you, Eli," he moaned.

Elijah pulled his mouth from him and climbed up, straddling his alpha. "I'm wet, Carter. Soaking."

Carter groaned and pulled him down for a kiss, hands cupping his ass, fingers wandering to his wet hole. One finger slid in, filling him tight.

"Oh god. Carter," he moaned, moving and rocking against his alpha. Carter slid another in, stretching him, taking his time.

Before long, Elijah couldn't take it anymore. In seconds, he was riding him, slowly filling with each movement up and down. It had been a very long time for him, and nothing had ever felt like this. Not like Carter.

Carter growled and flipped him, hiking his legs up. He moved faster and gripped Elijah's cock, stroking him.

Seconds later Elijah came, splattering Carter's hand and his stomach. A moment after, his alpha filled him with hot cum, shuddering and collapsing on top of him. They stayed like that for what seemed like forever, but dry cum wasn't comfortable.

After cleaning up, the two cuddled together, limbs entwined. Carter reached down and pulled the thick blankets up and over them. "Elijah," he said, voice soft and dazed.

"Hmm," was all he could manage. He felt so warm and cozy.

"I love you."

Elijah pulled his alpha close and laid his head on his shoulder. "I love you too," he said, after a moment. "More than I thought I could ever love a man."

Carter smiled joyfully, then fell asleep almost instantly. Elijah listened to the steady beat of his alpha's heart and the rain hitting the roof. He felt so much, so many things. Overwhelming things. They were together in this though. They'd make it.

Friday morning was the best morning of his life. He thoroughly enjoyed packing two lunches, one for Olive and one for Carter. He kissed Carter goodbye and hugged Olive, making sure she had her backpack. The two left in Carter's van, heading to town, one for school and one to install a new hot water heater.

"This is my life now," he told Hotdog and Winston as he plopped down on the couch. "Oh my God, this is my life now." He squealed, startling the two dogs.

He jumped up and danced through his chores, feeding and watering the animals, milking Pooka, cleaning out Hodges's cage. He checked his e-mails, answering student questions, then caught up on grading the discussion boards for his classes. He checked his investments, debating a new venture. Confidence high, he made it happen.

Around lunch time, after again feeding Billy, the baby goat, he decided to go into the store to see if they needed any help. He packed a crate of milk, loaded it in the Jeep, and made the short drive with Hotdog in tow. Winston was more interested in sleeping on Carter's pillow then coming along.

As was typical, Farm Fresh was packed with a nice mixture of locals and tourists. They would have a Halloween event next weekend, but the corn maze behind the store was up and going. It'd get busier at night, but it still had a nice crowd now.

He smiled when he saw Grammy's little Volkswagen bug parked in the back. He handed the milk off to Janelle, Aunt Anna's eldest, and went in search of his Grammy.

He walked through the crowds, nodding politely as he went, before finally turning into a hall and finding some quiet. The office door was cracked, and he could hear his Grammy's voice. He paused, about to enter, when her tone caught his attention. She sounded so sad and panicked.

"I just don't know what to do, Annie," Grammy said. "Your father and I wanted to buy the old Wright Mill and the acreage around it. We have the money, but Steven called and demanded a hundred thousand dollars. He's never asked for that much at once."

What the hell was his dad doing asking his Grammy

for that much money? His parents got a small stipend each month from the farm, because Gramps and Grammy insisted, but that was a lot of cash.

"Mama, you don't have to give it to him. He's gotten enough of our money over the years, and Elijah's an adult now. They can't take him away from us."

Elijah slowly sank down to the floor, back against the wall. He hugged Hotdog close to him. His parents had threatened to take him away from Gramps and Grammy? They had forced his grandparents to pay to keep him for years?

"He says they'll take Olive away. Sue for custody since Elijah's a single omega," Grammy said. He could hear in her voice that she was in tears. "They say he can't take care of her or provide for her, since he doesn't have a good job. He… He called him a *whore*, Annie. He called my little boy a whore."

Elijah froze in fear. They couldn't take his Olive. They *couldn't*.

"That's some complete and utter nonsense," Anna said. "You know, as well as I, that he takes real good care of that little girl. Town gossip is just town gossip."

"Of course he does, Annie," Grammy said, sniffling. "But you know how Steven can spin a story his way. How damn charming he can be when he wants. He'd paint the judge a picture of a single omega, teaching part-time, living off his family, and barely making ends meet."

"It's not about the truth with him, but what he can make others believe." Anna sounded defeated. "Damn that useless, cowardly, piece of shit."

Elijah's brows raised at his aunt's words. Anna hardly ever cursed. He took a deep breath and stood. He pushed the door open and walked in. Grammy and Anna jumped out of their chairs, looking guilty. Grammy's worn, kind face was covered in tears, but she wiped them away, struggling to smile. Her weak smile showed the little gap that she passed down to all of her children, grandchildren, and, so far, great-grandchildren.

"Hey there, baby boy. Did you come in to help with the store?" Her voice wobbled with suppressed tears.

"Grammy, Aunt Anna, we need to go see Gramps," he said firmly. "Now."

His aunt gave him a sad smile. "You hear us talking, Eli-baby?"

He hugged her tightly. "Yes, I did, and I'm only going to say my piece one time, so come on. Gramps needs to be involved."

"The store…" Anna started.

"Janelle can handle it. She has Fridays off from the library. Come on." He pulled the two women from the office and marched out the back.

"Janelle, we'll be back in a bit," he yelled as they made it to the door.

"You got it, tiger," she said. "Go get 'em."

He paused. "You know what's going on?"

"Not at all, but you look so fierce," the silly woman answered. "Grr."

"You are so weird, but I love you anyway." He rolled his eyes and continued out the door.

The three of them silently loaded up into Grammy's

car, and Anna drove up the hill toward his grandparents' house. Grammy was still crying, so Elijah hugged her close, reveling in her soft familiarity. Hotdog licked her face, making her chuckle. These two women had loved him unconditionally since the second he was born. He would do just about anything for them.

"Who's this little guy anyway? I didn't know you were getting another dog for Olive." Grammy petted Hotdog's soft ears.

"This is Hotdog. He's Carter's dog. Doc Grover found out my boyfriend's a giant marshmallow, so this is just one of our new pets. He also brought home a baby goat. Lord only knows what else we'll end up with."

Grammy and Anna laughed.

"When are we going to get to meet him," Grammy asked.

"This Sunday," Elijah said reluctantly. "Don't scare him off!"

The two women just rolled their eyes and smiled.

They arrived at the small house with a large barn in minutes. Though Grammy had said she wanted something smaller when she moved out of the farmhouse, she had still wanted plenty of space for Sunday breakfast and other holiday meals and get-togethers. That's where the barn came in.

They'd taken an old barn and renovated it into a large dining area with an attached kitchen. It had plenty of seating to relax and catch up with family. It was probably his favorite place in the whole world, aside from Carter's arms.

The three of them walked quietly into the house, and Gramps looked up from his paper, brows raised. His old hound dog, Rufus, lay at his feet. Hotdog immediately went to sniff the old dog, but Rufus just ignored him, snoring away.

"The three of you look like someone died. What's wrong?"

"Elijah heard me and Annie talking about Steven." Grammy sounded so dejected. She sat on Gramps' lap, head resting on his chest. She always said she liked to hear his heartbeat, because it made her feel safe.

Gramps stared hard at him. "Now, Elijah, that's nothing for you to worry about. Your father loves you. He just has some problems."

"No." Elijah wouldn't let Gramps keep protecting him. "I've known for a long time that neither mom nor dad give a damn about me. They didn't want an omega, but I don't care. When I was a kid… Yeah, it messed with me, but now? I've had the love of the two of you along with Aunt Anna and everyone else. I'm not a little boy wondering why his parents didn't want him. I know I'm loved."

"Oh, baby boy," Grammy said, fresh tears falling. "We didn't want you hurt for anything in the world."

"I know, Grammy, and I understand." He sat down roughly. "I had to tell Olive a few days ago about her bio alpha. It was hard, really hard. Her tears broke something in me."

"Oh dear," Anna said, sitting next to him and wrapping an arm around him.

"It sucks, but it is what it is. Family isn't always blood," he said. "Now this situation? It is mine to worry about. I don't want you giving anything to that bastard ever again. We have plenty of money, but it's money that we've earned, not him. He gets his stipend…"

"Not anymore," Gramps said. "If we aren't trying to keep him interested in the family for your sake, then he doesn't profit from the hard work of you and the others. Not anymore. We've given him more than enough through the years."

"Thank God," Elijah said. "I really dreaded having to cut the damn check for him, knowing he's been blackmailing you all my whole life."

"Trust me, it's bothered all of us," Anna said. "Marco got an effigy of Steven to torture when he signed that big contract with the chain of local grocery stores. He hated the idea of Steven's stipend increasing."

"Um, it didn't," Elijah said. "He hasn't gotten more than five hundred a month since I took over the books. As far as he knows, our farm hasn't grown as much as it has. Of course, I don't include him in the investments either. Noah, yes; my parents, no."

Gramps laughed. "Well, can't feel bad about that." He looked a bit sheepish. "I guess you'll be wanting the info on the account I pay him from, huh?"

"You know it, Gramps."

"I'm calling him today and telling him that you're seeing an alpha," Anna said. "That might throw him off."

"It could get rough, Elijah," Grammy said. "You don't know the things he's threatened throughout the years. He'll follow through on it too. He'll try to take Olive."

Elijah struggled to look calm and unafraid. "That's for me to worry about, Grammy. I'll take care of it."

CHAPTER 7

Carter finally finished up with his last client of the day. It had been a long damn day, especially for a Friday. He had the next two days off to spend alone with his omega. He still couldn't believe how good it had been last night. Sex was a simple process—insert Tab A into Slot B—but when love was involved? The simplest acts suddenly became the most profound.

He left Honey Buns with a big, steaming cup of coffee. A tall alpha leaned against his van. The man was handsome with blond hair and grey eyes. He was also a stranger.

"Can I help you?" Carter said, standing next to his door.

"You're dating Elijah Wilson, right?" The man looked a little sad.

"Yeah. You got a problem with that?" Carter hoped this didn't turn into another Mrs. Weber incident.

"No. Not at all," he said. "My name's Tanner. Tanner

Jones." He held his hand out, and Carter shook it. "I just wanted to make sure you know to take damn good care of that omega. You screw up and there's plenty of alphas willing and able to offer him a shoulder to cry on."

Carter frowned. "Trust me. I am not going to screw this up. He's the best thing that's ever happened to me, so you can take your shoulders elsewhere."

It was nice to know that not all the alphas in this town were idiots, but he didn't like the idea of them waiting on the sidelines.

"Good. He's a great guy." Tanner smiled self-deprecatingly. "I wish I would have figured that out when we were kids. You wouldn't have gotten a chance with him."

"Well," Carter said. "I'm glad you were a dumb kid? I guess? That seems rude, but I do really love my omega."

Tanner laughed. "I'm glad. Keep him happy, man. Oh, and can I make an appointment with you next week? Do you do tile? I know you're a plumber, but I have a tile job and can't find anyone local."

"I can do it. I worked with a lot of different craftsmen when I was training," Carter said, handing over a card. "Give me a call, and we'll set it up."

Tanner took it and left, walking down Main Street toward the high school.

His phone rang. "Yeah?" he answered, not recognizing the number.

"Stay away from Elijah Wilson," a woman's voice said. "A cripple like you could get hurt so easily."

"What the fuck? Are you threatening me?"

The call ended abruptly. What the hell had that been about?

His phone rang again. "What the hell do you want, lady?"

"Uh, hey man." Raymond sounded baffled and amused all at once.

"Oh, shit. Sorry, Ray. Some crazy person just called me. She threatened me, trying to get me to stay away from Elijah."

"What the hell? Want me to look into it? I can get your phone records and start the process to trace the call."

"I guess so. I'm not too worried about it, but it might be a good idea. Just make sure you charge me this time. I don't want you to get fired for doing free work."

"I'm so not charging you. Services here cost way too much. I'll do it on my down time, and you can just deal with it."

"Fine, fucker, but I'm definitely buying dinner next time we see each other."

"Sounds like a plan. Honestly, that may be sooner than you think. I found your omega's brother, and it's not good."

"Fuck, what's wrong?"

"His parents had him committed to a psychiatric hospital. Involuntarily and very much illegally. From what I can tell, they are in the process of trying to get access to his bank account now."

"How the hell could they do that? You said illegally?"

"Well, Noah was recruited to the army and finished OSUT about a year ago."

"Elijah didn't know. Wow, they really don't talk."

"His first deployment was six months ago."

"That was fast, but I know it happens that way sometimes. What happened?"

"He was only there for a week. An explosion injured him: fractured his skull and damaged his ears. As far as his medical records show, he's permanently deaf."

"Fuck, that's some bad luck."

"I know, right? A fucking week," Raymond said. "Well, his darling parents took him in when he finished the discharge process. A few days after that, he was in the St. Mercy's psych ward, north of Vegas."

"How do we get him out of there?"

"Family member signs him out. That's it. Bring a lawyer with you though. This place is a shithole."

"A lawyer. Shit. I can do that."

"Let me know when you go, and Juan and I will meet you out there. Offer some support."

"I'd appreciate that, but I'll try to fly out tonight. Elijah won't want him there all alone for longer than necessary. His cousin's already watching Olive for the next couple of days, so the timing is perfect. That doesn't give you enough time to plan, man, so don't worry."

"You do know I work from home, right?"

"You're working for that security firm. Don't they have you guarding people or something?"

"Man, I work with computers. I don't want to guard shit anymore. I didn't like hurting people while I was in the army. I'm not going to put myself in that kind of situation again if I can help it."

"Oh," he said, feeling like shit. "I'm so sorry, Ray. I need to listen better."

"Carter, do we often have deep conversations about our feelings?"

"No," he said, laughing.

"Then how would you know I have some issues rolling around in my head? Anyway, I'm definitely in for tomorrow. I know Juan will feel the same. Besides, what else would I be doing?"

"Um, having fun? Getting laid? Not helping me break my future brother-in-law out of a hospital?"

"Future brother-in-law, huh? It's that serious already?"

"Yes. I have the ring, and I moved in yesterday. I'm just waiting a little longer so I don't freak him out too much."

"I can't wait to meet him," Ray said, amused. "Has to be someone special to get you this involved so quickly."

They said goodbye, and Carter reluctantly made his next call.

"Hey, you said to call you if I needed something, right?" He hoped Caden had meant it.

AFTER BUYING tickets and reserving a room, Carter rushed home. He climbed the front steps, looking around. Elijah was usually cuddled in a chair on the porch at that time of day. It was colder, but they had a break from the rain.

He looked quickly through the large house but couldn't find him. They were supposed to spend time together tonight, right? Hodges was the only one in the house.

He walked out to the barn and knew something was terribly wrong right away. Boo sat at the entrance. She gave him a look telling him to get moving. Damn bossy cat.

He could hear sobbing from the door. Elijah was curled up in Billy's stall, Winston and Hotdog on either side of him. He held the baby goat in his arms, feeding him, and buried his face in his soft hair. His shoulders shook with his sobs.

Carter moved behind him, wrapping his arms around his omega. "Baby, what's wrong? Is it Olive? Is she okay? What can I do?"

His Elijah was supposed to dance and smile, not cry, never cry. Panic shot through him. It had to be Olive.

"She's fine," he said, struggling to stop crying. "It's just my parents."

"You know what those fuckers did to your brother? I just found out today."

He looked up, turning in his arms. He sat sideways on Carter's lap, still cuddling the damn goat. "Noah? They did something to Noah?"

Carter took a breath. "Okay, first, you tell me what they've done to upset you."

"Apparently, they've been blackmailing Gramps and

Grammy since I was a baby, threatening to take me away unless they gave them money."

"Those assholes."

"Yes," Elijah agreed, starting to cry again. "I hate the thought of causing Gramps and Grammy worry, even though I know it's not my fault. They were going to buy the old Wright Mill. Fix it up as a house and rent it out. They wanted the acreage that came with it, so Uncle Marco could get more cattle. Now, they won't even place a bid when I know we have the money."

"I'll make sure they get it, baby. I promise." Carter made a mental note to call his family's accountant. The guy would probably piss himself with joy that Carter wanted to use some of his trust fund.

"It's not really that, though that does suck," Elijah said, finally controlling his tears. "Today, I overheard Grammy talking to Aunt Anna. My father threatened to sue for custody of Olive if they didn't pay him a hundred thousand dollars."

"Seriously? That would never work. You're a great parent, and there would be no chance in hell of them winning."

"Grammy's not too sure, and I kind of agree with her. My dad has a way with words. He can twist the truth to be the way he wants it. I'm single, well sort of, and an omega. To his knowledge, I'm just a part-time teacher that mooches off the family."

"But that's not you. You work so hard every day. Plus, you have me. We were going to get joint accounts, and my business is doing well so far."

"Money's not that big of a deal. I invest a lot for the

farm and for my uncles and aunt. They wanted to set up accounts for each of my cousins. I personally have close to two million that I could access within a month, but my savings account is almost to a million too. Plus, the farm is doing really well, even without the investment fund I play with, but when you take it into account, we're talking over ten million."

"Well damn, I guess I need to turn over my trust fund for you to play with, huh?"

Elijah sniffled. "Well, if you're not using it, it's not helping you. You can at least use some to buy stocks."

Carter laughed. "My parents' accountant is going to love you."

Elijah managed a small smile, but it faded fast. "That doesn't change the fact that I'm an omega. Some people... Well, some don't like us much."

"They are complete idiots, but we can solve that problem really easily."

"How? I am who I am."

"Yeah, but we could get married, then you wouldn't be a *single* omega."

"Carter, no! I am not going to make you marry me. I already feel like I pushed you a bit to move in with me. I can't force you to tie yourself to me forever, and it *would* be forever. Fake marriage or not, if I get you, I'm not letting you go."

"It would very much not be a fake marriage, baby. I already got my great-grandmother's engagement ring sized. It's in a box in our closet. Trust me, if I didn't want to marry you, I wouldn't. Plus, according to

Tanner Jones, I better put a ring on you soon or some other alpha will steal you away."

Elijah started giggling. "You already sized the ring? How did you know my size? We've only been dating a month. Oh, my God!"

"Okay, so first, yes. I picked it up from the jeweler two weeks ago… Stop laughing at me. I knew where I wanted this to go the second I met you. Next, Zoe has told me your ring size at least once a day since I met her."

He watched his omega shake with laughter on the stall floor.

"If you don't stop laughing, you're going to drop Billy. Anyway, third, it has only been a month, but what did you tell me last night? You said 'why wait if you were so certain?' I feel the same. I've fallen for you, into you, since the second I laid eyes on you. No point denying it."

Elijah's laughter stopped, and he looked at Carter with big, wet eyes. It reminded him of the look Olive had given him that first day: adoring.

"So, we're going to get married," Elijah softly asked.

"Yes, in Vegas, tomorrow," he answered.

"Oh, my God, that's so soon. I need to get tickets, find someone to watch the house. Zoe has Olive, so there's that." He stood, placing Billy gently in the hay. He ran his hands through his dark curls, frowning.

"I already have the tickets and reserved a room. I can call Aunt Anna while you pack to see if one of her teens wants to stay here a day or two." He'd call his brother again too. Tell him the new development and get his advice.

"Wait," Elijah said. "You already have tickets?"

"Yeah." Carter sighed. This was going to suck. He quickly reviewed what Ray told him about Elijah's brother.

"Those bastards! Those… Those… I can't think of anything bad enough!" Elijah looked like he was about to murder someone.

"We're going to get him. We'll get married. Then we'll come home and plot revenge, okay?"

His omega shook with anger but nodded. "Yes, we will."

Elijah tapped his foot impatiently as they waited in the airport for the rest of their team. He was calling it the Super Fantastic Rescue Team. It was brilliant. His beautiful ring was also brilliant. It was vintage and covered in diamonds. He was a little afraid to wear it.

He'd told Zoe what was going on. After cursing up a storm, she insisted on bringing Olive to the wedding. Then she told Ernie, and he'd insisted on being there for Carter. What about his own *cousin?* Was Elijah chopped liver?

The wedding would be Sunday, at ten in the morning, so they had time to settle some things and get tickets. Zoe said she'd tell the family. That would go over so well. He hadn't even told anyone Carter had moved in.

"That's their flight," Carter said. "Juan and Ray should be out soon."

"Yes! Super Fantastic Rescue Team assemble," Elijah

said, throwing his arms in the air, admiring the glint of light off his ring.

"I think I'm just going to take this," Carter said and slowly grabbed Elijah's extra-large iced latte. It was his fourth in the past two hours, so maybe Carter had a point.

"Hey man, why you stealing that poor omega's coffee?" A warm voice boomed across the lobby. "It's two in the morning. He probably needs the caffeine to stay awake."

Elijah bounced on his toes. "You're Juan, aren't you? Carter told me that you had a green Mohawk, so I know it's you. I like your hair, but it wouldn't work on me. I dyed mine pink once in middle school, and it made me look way too delicate. Zoe called me Champagne for like a month afterward. It's my stripper name."

"Maybe taking the coffee was a good idea. He seems a bit wired," Juan said with a laugh. "It's nice to meet you, Elijah, and if you ever want to ditch Carter here, give me a call. You're adorable."

"Fuck man, don't steal Carter's sunshine. He's a complete asshole when he's grumpy, and you know it'd make him cry." Carter's other friend was a large, black man with kind brown eyes and a big smile. Elijah instantly loved him.

"Oh, my God, Carter, I love your friend Raymond. Look at those eyes and that smile! Can we keep him forever and ever? Can we? Can we?"

The three friends cracked up, and Juan took Elijah's

coffee from Carter and handed it back to him. "Man, you just keep drinking this."

Elijah rolled his eyes. "Come on, we have a brother to rescue!"

He darted off toward the car, humming the batman theme song. Carter and his friends followed behind him, still laughing. Holy guacamole, Carter's face when he laughed. Elijah wanted his friends to stay with them forever if they made him laugh like that. Relaxed and happy.

"A lawyer's meeting us there," Carter said as they climbed in the car. "I want to do this now, if you guys don't mind. I know it's late, but catching them off guard will be good, and Elijah's worried sick about him."

"No problem, man," Juan said. "Let's get this done."

Elijah wiggled in his seat and drank his coffee as they headed to the hospital. What if Noah really did need to be there? Maybe his parents had done what they thought was best for Noah, and he was just jumping to conclusions. He had to see Noah though. He'd know for sure then.

The hospital was a distance from Vegas, out in the desert. A large fence surrounded it, and a guarded entrance looked like the only way in. *That wasn't ominous at all*, Elijah thought.

A black SUV was parked at the gate, and two men got out of the car when they pulled alongside it. They were tall and looked very similar to Carter.

Elijah and the others got out of the car.

Carter nodded to the men. "Caden. Cain. I didn't expect you both to come. Thank you."

"Mother and Father are at the hotel," the older one, Caden, said. "If you're getting married, they wanted to be here."

Carter looked shocked to say the least. "You all flew out to Vegas within a few hours' notice?"

While Caden's face remained impassive, Cain looked vaguely surprised. "You and your omega are getting married. Why would we not come? Of course, it will be tacky, but we will endure."

Elijah gasped. "It will be tasteful!" He smiled, big and goofy. "I already planned it. It's perfect."

Carter smiled, pulling Elijah into his arms, and kissed him deeply. "Damn right, it'll be perfect. I'm marrying you."

"Oh fuck me sideways, that is too sweet," Juan said with a groan. "Yuck."

Ray elbowed his friend. "Don't be an ass."

Carter's brothers just stared at their younger brother.

They are so weird, Elijah thought. Like they were frozen and didn't know quite how to react to situations they didn't control.

"Let's do this," Elijah said, ready to see his brother. "Okay, lawyers, what's our approach?"

Cain's brow raised. "We do have names."

"Yes, and I know them. Your point?" Elijah raised his own brow, or at least tried to. He had a feeling it didn't look quite the same. Cain cracked a smile. "Fine, you can be part of the Super Fantastic Rescue Team. Cain. Caden. There! Are you happy?"

"Ecstatic," Cain said dryly.

"We've already spoken with the guard. The facility night manager is waiting inside," Caden said.

"Okay, let's go," Carter said. The group moved to their respective vehicles, and Elijah got in with Carter's brothers. Carter gave him a questioning look but shrugged and moved to the rental.

As the cars moved forward, Elijah spoke, trying to hurry. "I just want you guys to know that I'll take good care of Carter. I have a good savings, and the family's farm is doing really well. Olive and I love him, and we'll keep him happy. I promise."

"I ran a background check on you when Carter first told me about you," Caden said. "I am impressed with your financial choices. I know that you're not with Carter for his money. Mother and Father are not fully convinced, but Cain and I are."

"I knew when I saw the picture Carter texted Caden," Cain said. "He has never looked that happy." He looked back at Elijah, eyes steely. "Keep it that way."

Elijah grinned, which seemed to startle Cain. "I can't believe you just gave me the big brother speech. Oh my God, Carter is going to be so surprised." He paused. "Oh, and I will keep my alpha happy. No worries there."

Reaching the facility, the group walked in the front doors with Elijah and Carter in front, the lawyers on one side and the tough former soldiers on the other.

The night manager looked surprised for a moment, then hardened his expression.

"As I told your lawyers at the gate," he said, without waiting for introductions. "I can't possibly release a patient to someone I can't verify as a relative."

"As I told *you* at the gate," Caden said coldly. "We are here in an advisory capacity only, and we have the appropriate, notarized documentation proving our brother-in-law's relation to your patient." He handed him a folder. "In it, you will find birth certificates for both men. If you can take the time to read it, you will see that the parents are the same on each one."

How did he get our birth certificates, Elijah wondered.

"I hardly think three in the morning is a good time to be discussing…"

"Sir, now would be the perfect opportunity to do this," Ray said. "Would you really like potential patients and their families present to hear all the lovely things your *hospital* does to its patients? I've compiled a file here, if you'd like to take a look."

"Indeed, perhaps the police would like to come back with us," Cain said. "Then you can explain why you illegally committed an army veteran to a psychiatric hospital."

"It was not illegal. There is no need for the police to be involved. This is a place of healing," the man blustered. "His parents said…"

"His parents did not present a court order from a judge giving them permission to do anything on their son's behalf. The days of easy involuntary commitment to mental hospitals are long gone, sir," Caden interrupted.

"Maybe it was just a mistake," Juan said, smile understanding and sympathetic. "You just wanted to help the guy, but forgot to file the right paperwork? Now, his brother's here to take care of him. What's wrong with that?"

"Well, you may be right," the manager said. "It could just be an accident. Mistakes happen sometimes, and you do appear to have the correct documentation here." He finally gave in, sighing. "We'll go get him and bring him to you."

"No," Ray said. "We'll go with you to get him."

"Fine," the man said irritably.

The six of them followed the manager through the halls of the hospital. The plain white walls and floor creeped Elijah out. There was no screaming or any obvious signs of trouble, but the few patients in the halls were all a little too deferential to their orderlies. A little too quick to avoid their eyes.

They reached his brother's room, and Elijah immediately wanted to throttle the slimy little bastard beside them.

"He's very violent. We have to keep him restrained. We've kept him on some wonderful medication that helps. As you can see, he is quite calm and happy. Anytime it starts to wear off though… You should be careful as you tend to him," the manager said. "We'll write you a prescription before you go."

Elijah's nineteen-year-old brother lay strapped to the bed, eyes open, but mind clearly not there. He was hooked up to a catheter and IV. Face slack, drool spilled from the side of his mouth. "No," Elijah said firmly. "No medication."

"If you say so," the man said in disgust. "You're the one dealing with him now."

They quickly checked Noah out and moved him to the car, Juan carrying him. They laid him in the back seat and Elijah climbed in with him, putting his brother's head in his lap.

Ray smiled and insisted on riding with Carter's brothers, so they wouldn't be too cramped in the car. "I want to talk to them about what to do with this information I found on the hospital. The things they do to some of their patients is horrifying."

Elijah stroked his brother's short, black curls, grown out from their buzz cut. Freckles covered his nose, and hazel eyes stared up at him, unaware.

"Carter," he sobbed, tears falling.

His alpha reached his hand back from the front seat, and Elijah grabbed it. "He's going to be okay, baby. We'll figure this out. Get him anything he needs."

"I love you, alpha-mine."

"I love you too, baby."

A few hours after they settled in their hotel room, Noah's medication started to wear off. He was confused, scared, and would only stay calm when he saw Elijah. He clung to his brother, crying. Elijah wasn't much better. He wouldn't leave him, even dragging Noah to the bathroom when his omega wanted a shower.

Carter could only imagine what the young man was going through. The injuries he'd sustained were bad enough, but to arrive home only to be forced into a constantly drugged state of captivity? Noah was only a kid, nineteen. Carter couldn't wait to see the brothers' parents pay.

By noon, though, reality set in, and Noah seemed to realize that he was safe. There was absolutely nothing wrong with him mentally. There had been no reason to commit him beyond his parents' desire to get to the money he had saved from his much larger stipends from the farm.

He couldn't hear, but he did a decent job reading lips, and, of course, he could still speak. He just misjudged his volume sometimes. The young man seemed obsessed with vibrations though. He liked to put his hand on Elijah's throat when he spoke, watching his lips and *feeling* the words.

After a couple of hours, Noah did the same to him. It was strange, but it made Carter damn happy. It meant the young alpha trusted Carter, at least a little.

Elijah and Noah finally fell asleep together in one of the two king-sized beds, and Carter knew it was time to face the beasts waiting for him down in the hotel restaurant. He was tired, but he was used to going without sleep. He'd sleep again when he got home. An intense longing hit him as he thought of home.

He could already see himself curled up on the couch with Elijah and Olive, Juan and Ray watching the game on the TV, being their normal dumb selves. Noah was there, somewhere. He'd fit eventually, Carter knew it. He couldn't see his parents or brothers there though. The image of the old farmhouse and his family didn't compute.

He found them sitting at a table by the window, looking out at the Vegas Strip. His parents sat together on one side of the table. He sat down on the other. His father looked as crisp and well-pressed as usual in a pair of dress pants and a plain white button-down shirt. His mother coolly assessed him from her seat, her designer dress impeccable.

"Carter," she said. "Are the boys alright?" Her words

surprised Carter. Caden had said they were concerned about him marrying Elijah, so he'd fully expected a lecture on choosing a *more appropriate* omega. Just like the lecture about choosing an *appropriate* college and career.

"Noah's medication wore off, and he's aware. Knows he's safe, but needs Elijah nearby. They finally fell asleep about an hour ago."

"He texted me earlier about appropriate apparel for the wedding. I asked if he needed anything for it, and he asked for few things. Here they are, so don't forget them when you go back up," she said, gesturing to a large, plain black shopping bag next to the table.

"He texted you?"

"Yes, Carter. Some young men realize that a lady may worry about what to wear to a themed wedding. I *will not* stick out like a sore thumb in the pictures."

His father grinned at him. Grinned! "Do you know what he has planned?"

"No, I let him plan everything for it. Told him to just put what he wanted me to wear on the bed, and I'd be good to go."

"Well, we'll let it be a surprise then," his mother said, amused.

"Carter," his father said. Ah, here came the lecture. "Your omega seems like a wonderful person. We're so happy for you."

Shock froze him for a moment, then anger bubbled up, though he knew it was irrational. He had twenty-eight years' worth of it, twenty-eight years of being their disappointment.

"What? You've never been happy with anything I've ever done."

His father winced and looked away.

His mother sighed. "Carter, we realize that we have been far too critical toward you. We wanted what we thought was best for you, but to be honest, we forgot to think of *you* in that process."

"As long as you are happy, son, then we are," his father said, looking tired and sad. "When you were injured, the doctors couldn't tell us if you would live or not. It was... It was quite frightening. Your commanding officer explained what had happened, and it became perfectly clear that we did not know a damn thing about you. When I pictured you as a soldier, I pictured you drinking away your time, flirting with all the uniform groupies."

"We didn't realize the reality of it—that we could lose you—until then," his mother said. "Then when you came back, you were so broken in spirit and body. We were so worried, but we didn't know how to talk to you, to comfort you. When Caden sent everyone that picture you texted him, we saw what you should be, where you should be. We saw you smile, son. It has been so long since I saw you smile. We do love you, darling, even if we didn't show it very well through the years."

Carter didn't know how to feel. He was happy, so damn happy, that his parents were saying this. But twenty-eight years? It took that long? A warm hand on his shoulder startled him, but he instantly felt calmer. Elijah.

His omega looked sleepy and rumpled. "Hey alpha-mine, I got hungry," he said, taking the chair next to him. "Juan and Ray are staying with Noah, so he's not alone." He took hold of Carter's hand and looked his parents over. "You must be Mr. and Mrs. Benson. I'm so sorry that we haven't met before now."

Carter's mother smiled. "Please, call us Susan and John. It's an odd situation, but that is life, isn't it? Now, darling, do you need any help with the wedding. You look absolutely exhausted, and I would be more than happy to help."

Elijah smiled, relieved. "My cousins Zoe and Ernie just arrived at the airport with my daughter. I know Zoe would love to help too, but it's a lot. If I made a list, would you mind helping her?"

"Wait, Ernie and Olive are here?" Excitement coursed through him. He hadn't realized how much he missed his favorite girl and his new best friend. "Come on, let's go get them," he said, voice scratchy and rough. He really did need to rest, but he started to rise from his seat.

Elijah laughed. "Sit down, Softie McSoftster. I need food, and Zoe's going to rent a car." He smiled at Carter's parents. "Olive has him wrapped around her little finger, and apparently, Ernie's his new best friend."

Susan smiled softly, a bit of longing in her eyes. "Could Olive come with Zoe and me? I promise I would keep a close eye on her."

Elijah snorted. "You just try to keep her away. She's

super excited about the wedding. Keeps telling me 'I told you so.'"

"Well, she did tell you to marry me a long time ago. You should have listened better." Carter smiled smugly.

"Really? A long time ago was last week. Hold on, you are the one who had my beautiful engagement ring sized two weeks ago, so maybe last week really is a long time for you."

"Stop laughing at me, jerkhead. You were the one who asked me to move in last week."

"Children," Susan said, laughter in her voice. "Do behave."

"Fine," Elijah sighed.

The four had a quick breakfast, and the conversation flowed between the two couples. Carter couldn't remember ever having an actual conversation with his parents like this. As they were finishing up, Caden and Cain sat at the table. They both looked sleepy and quickly ordered some coffee.

"Susan, would you mind coming up to our room with me? I'd like to check on Noah and make that list."

"Of course, Elijah," she said. She rose from her seat, all grace and beauty, and picked up her shopping bag.

Elijah hugged Carter and kissed his cheek. "See you in a bit, alpha-mine. Make sure you get some sleep today. You aren't superhuman. Keep an eye out for our girl. She'll be here soon."

"Got it, baby." He watched his omega walk away, enjoying the view.

"If you can drag your eyes over here, Carter, we can

discuss your situation a bit." Caden's voice was as serious as usual, but his lips curved in a small smile.

Carter blushed. "Yeah, sorry about that."

His father snorted. "For some reason, I don't think you're really sorry."

Carter grinned. Yeah, he wasn't. His mate was hot.

"So, as for Noah's situation, we need to file a restraining order against his parents and then get him out of here. After speaking with Raymond last night, we sent the information he gathered on St. Mercy's to the police. They'll be by to talk with Noah today at two," Cain said. "That should be enough to justify the restraining order. We have found a good lawyer here in Nevada that will keep an eye on the situation, so Noah does not have to stay."

"Unfortunately, we are not licensed to practice in this state, but we are in Maine, so it would be best if you were to take Noah home with you," his father said. "We can offer our own brand of protection there."

"That's our plan… Wait, you said you're licensed to practice in Maine? Since when?"

"Well, when you moved, we all started the process," Caden said. "Fortunately, the timing was just right."

"We may not be former army buddies," Cain said. "But we have some skills that might be useful."

Was Cain bothered by his closeness to Ray and Juan? His brother's jealousy made Carter grin.

"Anyway, Noah's situation will be a lengthy process to deal with. Proving his parents did anything illegal will take a little time, and Elijah's situation is more immediate," Caden said.

"While marrying just to prove an omega is stable is truly ridiculous, in this case, it is the quickest and easiest route to immediate safety for Olive. We did some digging into Steven Wilson's background, and it is truly alarming. The man is a con artist, and that wife of his is not much better." John frowned and took another sip of his coffee. "Rachael Wilson has managed to collect quite a few expensive 'gifts and favors' from some very powerful men. I suspect sexual favors are exchanged with full approval from her husband."

"Fuck, that's horrible," Carter said. "The more I learn about these people, the more surprised I am they managed to create Elijah. I planned on marrying my omega anyway, but if it helps Olive, we're both happy to speed up the process."

"Papa!" Olive's voice boomed through the hotel restaurant. He just managed to get to his feet before he had an armful of Olive. The little girl wrapped her legs around his waist and her arms around his neck. "I missed you so much. Daddy said you was getting married, so now you'll stay forever and ever."

"Hey, baby girl," he said. "I missed you too."

"Whoa, that girl can run," Ernie said, panting as he reached the table. "She saw you and took off."

"Ernie," Carter said. "Glad you could make it."

"Of course, I could make it." He shrugged and looked around the table. "I take it these men are your family? You all look alike."

"Yes, this is my father, John Benson, and my two brothers, Caden and Cain." Ernie grinned and plopped into a seat. "Guys, this is Ernie and my darling Olive."

"He's your daddy, Papa? That means he's mine too, right?" Olive watched Carter's father and brothers with interest, plotting her takeover.

"Oh, yeah. He's like Gramps."

"Can I call you Pops? Shelly calls her papa's daddy Pops."

Carter's father grinned with pleasure. "You certainly may."

Olive clapped with happiness, giggling. "And you guys are my uncles? I have an Uncle Noah, and now I have two more?"

Caden nodded seriously. "Yes. Uncle Caden and Uncle Cain. I will, of course, be your favorite, but that is as it should be."

"You are mistaken," Cain said, equally serious. "I will be her favorite."

Olive's giggles turned to loud laughter. "Don't fight! I'll love you all equally. You can all be my favorite."

The two men smiled at their niece, completely charmed.

Yep, the girl owned them all.

CHAPTER 10

"Okay, we can do all that," Zoe said. "Now you and Noah need to rest." Elijah's cousin sat at Noah's side, gently stroking the young man's hair. "Poor boy had to deal with those assholes his whole life. He has us now."

"From what John has said, your parents really are rather awful." Susan perched on the chair at the window, reviewing Elijah's list. "However, your extended family sound absolutely lovely, and you both have the Bensons now too."

Elijah smiled, pleased with how Carter's family turned out. He had been fully prepared to kick some lawyer butts, but he was happy he didn't have to. He was already attached to Susan, so he hoped the Benson men could deal with one another. He wasn't giving her up.

Zoe sat beside him, grabbing his hand. "You do know that Grammy and Aunt Anna are already planning a big wedding, right? They're thinking May."

"I thought that might happen. I know this wedding is about convenience and protecting Olive, but you know I've fantasized about this for years. This wedding will be *my* wedding."

"Any wedding you have should be yours," Zoe said. "Do you want me to tell them to lay off the second wedding?"

Susan laughed. *Even her laughs are melodious and perfect*, Elijah thought in amusement. Carter's mom was just about the most beautiful and graceful woman he had ever seen, equal only to Grammy and Aunt Anna, of course. "Weddings are never just about the couple, unfortunate as that is. If it was, then there would be many more elopements."

Zoe snorted. "You have a point. Well, in any case, they are not too happy with you. You haven't even let them meet Carter yet. They're planning this big thing for him at the Halloween Bash next weekend." She started giggling. "It's really kind of awesome."

"Once we're married, he's mine forever, so you all can meet him then. He won't be able to run."

"You do know people divorce all the time, right?" Zoe looked concerned. "I know you're a bit naïve, but marriage doesn't make everything perfect."

"I know," he said. "Nothing's really perfect, but me and Carter? We're great together. Marriage just finalizes it. Carter and I will make it work, no matter what." His scratched his stomach. It had been itching all day.

"Do you need some lotion, sweetie," Susan asked. "You've been scratching at your stomach all morning."

Zoe's eyes widened. "Let me see that belly!" She tackled Elijah and tried to roll him on the bed.

"Back off, woman," Elijah yelled, trying to push her off him.

Noah sat up, looked at the two of them wrestling on the bed, and rolled his eyes. He smiled shyly at Susan. She nodded politely and made sure to enunciate as she spoke so he'd stand a better chance of reading her lips. "Hello, Noah."

"Hah, got you!" Zoe sat on top of him and forced his t-shirt up. She looked at his belly as he rolled, stuck like a turtle on his back. "Oh my God!" Her shriek surely woke the dead. Zombies would eat them all now. He would die first, he knew it. He ran too slowly. *Fair thee well, Carter my love. Protect Olive.* "Susan, look at this!"

Susan raised a brow but came to look at Elijah's exposed stomach. Her smile lit up the room, and her eyes watered. "Oh, Elijah," she said, tears falling.

"What? Do I have a tumor," he asked.

Noah looked over the women's shoulders. "You're pregnant," he said loudly.

"What! How's that possible? What!" He'd only had sex with Carter twice—their first time, then a quickie on the plane, because Elijah had always wanted to do that. It had been very uncomfortable.

"Well, when an alpha and an omega like one another, they go to their room for a private dance," Zoe said sarcastically.

"Are you the one who told Olive that's how babies are made?"

"Would you rather I tell her the truth?

"No, but why did you include Santa?"

"I didn't say anything about Santa."

"Then why did… Never mind, it's not important, because I'm freaking pregnant."

"Two grandbabies," Susan said, crying. She even cried beautifully. "Your omega line is pink and swollen. Nine months and we'll have a little baby."

"Oh, fuck a duck," Elijah said. He could feel his panic rising. What would Carter think?

"Are you not happy, sweetie?" Susan sounded baffled. "You love Olive so much, so I thought…"

"No," Elijah wailed. "I'm so damn happy, and I want Carter right now so I can tell him, but Zoe's big butt won't let me up."

His cousin gasped in outrage. "My butt is not big, you jerk." She sniffed. "Plus, if I get up, you'll just lock yourself in the bathroom and freak out."

"Yeah, so? What's it to you?" A little freak out never hurt anyone.

"So," she said. "I'll go get your honey, and Susan can sit on you. You two need to bond anyway."

"I really need to sit on him?"

"Yes," Zoe answered. "Or he will be in the bathroom for the rest of the night."

Carter's mom sighed, then hopped on his legs, scooting when Zoe moved to take her place. She crossed her legs and placed her hands in her lap. "This is so strange."

"Be right back!" Zoe ran out the door.

Noah came out of the bathroom, hair combed. He patted Elijah on the head as he walked by. He rummaged in Elijah's suitcase, pulled out a fresh shirt and some jogging pants, then turned around and went back into the bathroom.

"I hope he'll be okay," Elijah said, sighing.

"Oh, sweetie," Susan said. "He will be. He has you. Now, why are you so nervous?"

"I'm worried Carter will think it's too much, too fast. We just moved in together a couple days ago, and now we're getting married to help Olive. Where's a baby fit in there?"

"Carter absolutely adores you, darling. Is this all a little fast? Of course it is, but sometimes it works like that."

"What about my parents? They'll try to use this against us."

"Oh, you just let my husband and sons deal with that garbage. We will all keep you and Olive safe."

Carter, along with all their friends and family, piled into the room. Noah came out of the bathroom and sat in the chair, smiling in amusement.

"Susan, why are you sitting on our son-in-law," John asked.

"Oh, it seemed like the thing to do at the time," she answered. "Carter, darling, look at your omega's belly."

"I love his belly," Carter said laughing. His laughter stopped when he saw Elijah's omega line. His eyes grew big and wet. "Elijah, does that mean what I think it means?"

"Nine months from now, we'll have a baby, Carter," Elijah said.

"Yay! Santa's coming," Olive said, dancing around.

"Huh?" Juan asked.

Ernie rolled his eyes. "Don't ask."

"Hey, Ernie," Elijah said, trying to distract a room full of people from staring at his belly. "Thanks for coming out to stand with me tomorrow. It means a lot."

"Oh," Ernie said. "Wow, so this is awkward. Uh, Elijah, I'll be standing with Carter."

"What!"

Carter grinned. "We're best friends, baby. I've told you that like twelve times."

"Best friends forever, Daddy," Olive said. "He said so lots of times."

"What about Juan and Ray? They're your friend quota."

"Yeah, they're standing with me too. I have three best friends," Carter said and shrugged.

"Fine! I'm taking Cain and Caden, then. They're mine now!"

"Baby, they're my brothers. They would need to stand with me too."

"No! They're mine now."

"You have Zoe and Noah."

"And now I have Caden and Cain too. They're mine. Mine, mine, mine."

"Daddy," Olive said. "Sharing is caring."

"Yes, and papa is going to share his brothers with me, because they're mine now."

"Oh, sweetie," Susan said. "How about this: Carter

gets Ernie, Ray, and Caden. You can have Zoe, Juan, and Cain. Olive will be the flower girl, and Noah will walk you down the aisle."

Elijah sighed heavily. "Fine. Juan has a cool mohawk, and Cain can show me how to do the eyebrow thing."

"I feel like a piece of meat," Juan said.

CHAPTER 11

Carter stared down at his outfit for the wedding. "Um, baby, is this a Han Solo costume?"

"Yes, now hurry up and put it on. We have less than an hour left to dress and get to the park," Elijah called from the bathroom.

Noah came out dressed as Luke Skywalker, lightsaber included. He grinned at Carter. "I love my brother, but he is so weird." Noah was getting more comfortable with talking aloud, but he did struggle a bit at reading lips. He was working on it though.

Olive came out of the bathroom dressed like an Ewok. She was absolutely adorable with a little black painted nose. "Hurry up, Papa," she said. "Hey, Uncle Noah, I got us a book to read together." She went to her backpack and pulled out a large book. Running over to her uncle, she held it up. "See, we can learn sign language together."

Noah's eyes grew wet, and he smiled brightly at his

niece. "Thank you, Olive." He took the book and held it close to his chest. Carter really loved his little girl.

"Carter, get in there and get dressed," Elijah said, finally coming out of the bathroom. He was dressed in a traditional Princess Leia costume, a long, white hooded dress with a wide silver belt and white boots. Carter grinned. Elijah even had the wig to go with it. He looked as adorable as Olive.

"Do I look okay?" he said shyly. "Your mom bought a really high quality costume. Zoe said she refused to settle for less than perfect. I feel so beautiful."

"Baby, you are stunning," Carter said and grabbed his costume. "I'll hurry, then we can get moving. Where is the wedding?" he asked as he hurried to the bathroom.

"Red Rock Canyon," Elijah answered. "The limo will be here to pick everyone up in about thirty minutes."

After dressing, they went to wait for the others in the hotel lobby. Their family and friends trailed in, and Carter couldn't help but feel so damn happy when he saw each one had fully committed to making Elijah's dream wedding a reality.

Juan was dressed as Poe Dameron and Ray as Lando Calrissian. Ernie was dressed as Chewbacca and Zoe as Rey.

"I had to fight Juan for the Chewbacca costume," Ernie said. He did his Wookie call and grabbed Olive, tickling the giggling girl.

"Chewbacca's the best," Juan said. "But I make this leather jacket look good."

"So modest, guys, really."

Zoe sighed as she looked longingly at Elijah's costume. "You look so beautiful, Elijah, but that dress must really be hot. We can switch costumes anytime you want."

Elijah snorted and glared at his cousin. "Don't try to play me for a fool, Zozo. You can be Princess Leia in your own wedding."

She stomped her foot and huffed. "Fine."

Caden and Cain came down together. Caden was dressed as Kylo Ren and Cain as Darth Maul, full make-up included. Carter couldn't stop grinning. He had never seen his brothers in anything other than suits or polo shirts. They looked so uncomfortable. It was great.

"Aww, why didn't I think of Darth Maul," Juan said, then his eyes widened. "Holy shit, Carter, your mom looks hot."

"Never let me here those words come out of your mouth again, Juan," Carter said, gagging.

Caden and Cain both groaned.

"Never, never again," Cain agreed.

Carter's mother was dressed as Queen Amidala, headdress and make-up included. She looked exquisite. Carter's dad was dressed as Darth Vader. At least, he thought that was his dad. It could have been anyone really.

"Are you ready to get married, son?" Yep, that was his dad.

"I'm more than ready," he answered, grinning at his friends and families. "Please tell me someone is going to take pictures."

"Of course, darling," his mother said. "I hired a professional photographer. He'll be meeting us, along with the minister, at the venue. Now, here are your flowers, Elijah. You look so beautiful."

"Thank you, Susan. Everything is more than I expected. You and Zoe went above and beyond. I really appreciate it," Elijah said.

"Oh, dork," Zoe said. "You are so worth it. Come on. Let's lock this sucker in before he figures out what he's getting into."

"Classy, Zoe," Ernie said, snorting. "Classy."

They piled into the large limo, passing around the champagne or—in Olive's and Elijah's cases—the sparking white grape juice. Elijah clutched his bouquet of a large collection of wildflowers. His eyes were dreamy and his smile sweet. It more than made up for having to wear an elaborate costume in eighty degree weather.

Once there, the minister, dressed as Yoda, stood out among the rocks, dirt, and brush. He was under a rough wooden arbor decorated with wildflowers. Several rough wooden boxes of various sizes dotted the area, filled to the brim with a small variety of cacti and wildflowers.

The photographer silently snapped pictures, almost invisible.

All Carter could see was his omega, smiling and happy, joy shining in his eyes. His pregnant omega.

Their friends and family lined up, and Noah escorted Elijah to Carter, smiling softly. The ceremony went quickly.

"In a galaxy, far far away…" the minister began. The rest of his words were a blur, Carter's attention stuck on his omega.

Elijah smiled, the gap in his teeth causing Carter's heart to beat faster. Somehow, he managed to stutter, "I do," and they were married. Elijah was his.

They were separated and hugs were passed around. Then the photographer gave her orders, and everyone spent an hour posing for pictures, the beautiful scenery making a nice backdrop. Not a single person complained, despite the heat. Elijah practically glowed, enjoying every second.

Back in the limo, Carter's mom passed out ice-cold glasses of water. "Elijah, darling, I'm having your decorations, including the arbor, shipped to Maine, but I hope you don't mind if a keep a few cacti to remember the day."

Elijah grinned. "That sounds just perfect. All of this was just perfect."

That's what Carter liked to hear his omega say.

Carter watched his omega arrange his new cacti around the sunroom. He hummed and swayed as he arranged the photos from the wedding around the plants in the room. He didn't think Elijah would ever come down from his wedding high.

The sunroom was Elijah's favorite room in the house. It was full of houseplants, bookcases, and comfortable chairs. There was one loveseat against the wall they had enjoyed together earlier in the morning while Olive was still asleep.

Hotdog tugged on his rope, drawing Carter's attention. "When do I need to be at the party tonight?" The Wilson's Halloween Bash was that night, and it would be the first time he met Elijah's full family. Nervous didn't even begin to describe how he felt.

"In about an hour. Is Olive out of the bath yet? I need to get her over there so she can get dressed in her costume."

"And I'm not allowed to see her costume or yours?"

"Nope," he said. "You have to wait. Don't worry. You'll be getting there before we open to the public."

"Hmmpf," he grunted. "I guess I'll wear my Solo costume tonight."

"You will not!" Elijah looked affronted. "That is your wedding suit. You don't just wear that around. I set out a costume for you on the bed."

"I saw that one. I don't want to be a lumberjack."

"I'm sorry, but that's my fantasy of you. What can I say? I'm from Maine, and you have this nice beard now."

"Fine," he sighed. "For you."

"Daddy, come on," Olive said, carrying Winston. The small dog was dressed as a professor with a tweed coat and glasses.

Hotdog abandoned the rope and ran to them. He was dressed as a... Well, as a hotdog.

"Alright, baby girl. Let's go." Elijah kissed him. "I love you so much, and I'll see you there."

They left, and Carter went to get dressed. Reluctantly, he pulled on his costume. At least, it was comfortable, even if he looked like Paul Bunyan.

After a short drive, he arrived at Farm Fresh. Several cars were parked outside, but the place was eerily quiet. Getting out, he slowly approached the door. Fog eased out of the bottom, telling him they had the fog machine going already. He slowly opened the door and stepped inside. Fog pooled on the floor and black lights gave him a creepy feeling.

Looking around, the place appeared empty, but Carter had a bad feeling. Suddenly, a figure rose from behind a display. A ghost clown. The figure's white face was zombified, blood dripping from the knife in his head.

After the first one appeared, staring at him in silence, another one popped up, then another and another. Soon enough, the entire room was full of ghost clowns. He started to laugh.

The smallest one and another approached him, and Carter instantly recognized Olive and Elijah.

"You said you'd stay even if my whole family were ghost clowns," Elijah said solemnly. "Well, here they are."

"I'm not running, baby."

An older ghost clown couple stepped forward. "Hi, Carter," the woman, Grammy, said. "We're so happy to finally meet you."

The male ghost clown pulled him into a hug. "Come here, son. You have no idea how happy you've made us. Our little Elijah has finally found his joy." He pulled back. "You."

Grinning, Carter met each of Elijah's family members. His uncles Marco and Barry and their husbands. His Aunt Anna, who he'd already spoken to, and her large, quiet, beta husband. The petite woman hugged him tightly, surprisingly strong.

Then each of his cousins, even the one that was in college, introduced themselves.

"Sorry we haven't met before," Harper, a large alpha, said. "Unlike Uncle Barry's group, my dad and Aunt Anna's kids actually respected Elijah's order to stay away from you. Now, though, you're stuck. Sorry, man."

"Hey, is Hotdog yours?" The youngest, Hannah, bounced on her feet, holding Hotdog. She made an adorable ghost clown.

"Yeah. He's my first pet. Do you like him?"

"He's the best," she said. "If you need anyone to dog sit, let me know, kk?"

"You got it."

"So, how do you like the family so far," Ernie asked after Carter had met everyone.

"You guys are the best. I can't believe you did all of this."

"We had to make you feel welcome. I don't think you get how happy you make Elijah. He was content before, making his way through life and taking care of Olive, but he wasn't happy. You, my friend, make him happy."

"Well, he makes me happy too, so we're even."

Other guests arrived, filling the store up. Most of the townspeople tried to come to any of the events that the Wilsons planned, and the Halloween Bash was no exception.

"Papa, can you take me through the Haunted House? Daddy's too scared." Olive grabbed his hand, not waiting for an answer, and dragged him outside the store.

"You got it, sweet girl," he answered, laughing.

They walked through the house, Olive's eyes big and moving all over the rooms. He barely heard the couple behind him over the loud, spooky music, but he did hear them.

"I hope it works out for him," the woman told her friend. "He really is a sweet guy, but he gets a lot of shit for being an omega."

"I don't know, Jeanie. He's an unwed omega with a kid. Why would a successful guy like Benson want to stay with him? I mean, I hope he does, but does it seem likely? You know how people feel about him."

"Well, people can be stupid. Mr. Bartley told me this new guy is nice and doesn't have his head up his ass, so he should be able to see how awesome Elijah is."

The two girls laughed and fell behind the rest of the crowd. Carter didn't especially like that people were gossiping about Elijah, but at least, those two girls didn't think poorly of his omega.

"Pumpkin carving contest," Olive screamed. She abandoned Carter and ran after Grammy.

"Sorry, man," Elijah's seventeen-year-old cousin, Shawn, said. "Grammy carves the best pumpkins, and Olive likes to win. Want to partner up?"

Carter grinned. "Let's do it."

Milly and Gramps settled beside them with their own pumpkin. "We're gonna kick your butt, Shawn," Milly said.

Gramps laughed. "Show some good sportsmanship, pumpkin."

"It's just Shawn. I don't have to be nice to him."

"I wouldn't know what to do if she was, Gramps," Shawn said.

"I guess loving to annoy each other is still loving," Gramps said with a laugh.

The whistle blew, and the contest was on. Twenty minutes later, Carter and Shawn had a decent picture of Elvis carved into their pumpkin.

Gramps and Milly had carved a nasty looking witch. Gramps leaned closer to Shawn and Milly. "That's your Grammy when I don't take my boots off coming into the house."

They all snickered, and Grammy turned their way, suspicious. Their laughter died off, and they all tried their best to look innocent. Carter had the feeling Grammy hadn't bought it.

They didn't win. They didn't even come close to winning, but they had a lot of fun. Grammy and Olive won with their perfectly detailed Halloween scene carved into a large pumpkin. When the contest was over, he looked around for his omega, finally finding him grazing at the buffet table.

"Hey, baby," he said, kissing Elijah's neck, tickling him with his beard.

Elijah giggled and leaned into him. "Having fun? I've been eating since we got here. I swear I've never been so hungry in my life."

"You're eating for two, babe. Don't worry about it and eat all you want," he said.

Zoe moaned. "Why can't I hear those words from anyone I date?"

"Because you date douchebags," Janelle said. The younger woman was a little flaky, but according to Elijah, she was always honest.

"This is true," Zoe agreed.

Carter watched his husband stuff his face with cookies and grinned. He had a damn good life.

Later that night, he held his panting, sweaty omega after taking him from behind. Carter held him close, face buried in his neck.

"I don't know what I'd do without you, Eli," he said. "Thank you for loving me."

"Oh, Carter," Elijah said, turning in his arms and kissing his cheek. "You have nothing to thank me for, I promise. I am a selfish, selfish bastard. You'll never get away from me now, alpha-mine. I love you."

Carter smiled. "I know."

"Oh, you bastard! Quoting Han to me." Elijah laughed and rolled him to his back. "You get me."

"You know you don't have to bake for the store too when you get a craving, right?" Anna asked.

Elijah worked on mixing the dough for the walnut bread he was baking, shaking his butt and humming a song. Over the last few weeks, cravings had hit him hard. All he wanted was bread, all types of bread, but at least sales had been up at Farm Fresh since he'd started his frenzy of baking.

"Noah and I finished harvesting the orchard last week and Grammy's cranberries a few days ago. I have more time than usual and want to be productive," he said. Winston yawned from his doggy bed in the corner, and Hotdog had yet to stop running around the table.

Aunt Anna sat at the table in the kitchen loft, resting her feet after the busy morning. "I can't believe my Eli-baby's pregnant again."

She smiled happily and flipped another page in the

wedding magazine she was reading. "Are you sure you're alright with mom and me planning the wedding? I know you got your dream wedding last month, but we really don't want to step on your toes."

"Bah, Carter and I don't care," he said. "I want a wedding with all of you there, and if it makes you happy to plan it, well, lucky me."

They hadn't made it public knowledge that they were married, but the whole town knew he wore Carter's ring. As far as he was concerned, that's all he needed.

She smiled and flipped another page. "I'm glad. We're having a blast. Did you hear back from Mrs. Benson about Thanksgiving? It's only a week away."

"Yes! I texted Grammy this morning. Susan said they would be able to make it. I can't believe they're going to fly all the way up here for Thanksgiving. Olive is super excited. She misses her Mimi and Pops."

"That little brat has a way of wrapping everyone around her little finger. Myself included."

Elijah laughed. "True."

"How's Noah doing? I don't see him around much. We're trying not to push him too much, but the time's coming that he's going to have to deal with our meddling. It's part of being family."

"I'm surprised you all lasted this long, honestly." Elijah poured the mixture into the pans, seven this time, and popped them in the oven. He sat across from his aunt. "Noah is actually doing really well. The VA doctor said his hearing is gone for good, but otherwise, he is in good health. He was really lucky that he didn't die."

"Can they not do anything about his hearing? Technology's a crazy thing."

"With him being an adult, there's just too many risks. He chose to not attempt them. At least for now."

"Well, the family's been working on learning sign language. We each practice separately and together as we have time. Marco's gotten really good at it, the bastard. I don't know if my fingers will ever get the hang of it."

Elijah laughed. "We've been working on it too. Noah and Olive are the best, but Carter and I are learning, just slower."

"Elijah Bartholomew Wilson!" Grammy's voice rang from the bottom of the stairs. He could hear her stomping up the wrought iron steps.

"Uh oh," Anna said. "Someone's in trouble."

Grammy reached the top and stomped over, standing in front of him, hands on her hips. "What's this I hear about you and Carter buying the Wright mill and land? Marco said he received a deed to the acreage in the mail in his name."

Elijah smiled sheepishly. "Surprise?"

"Elijah!"

"Fine," he said, groaning. "Carter bought it the same day we left for Vegas. I told him what you all wanted it for, so he made sure it happened. He has the deed for the mill too, but he wants to talk to you all about it."

Grammy sat down. "We could have bought that, Elijah. Ya'll have a baby on the way."

"Grammy," Elijah said. "Carter bought that with money from his trust fund. A trust fund with over a million dollars in it since I took some out and invested it. We have plenty of money."

"That's not the point. That's your money, and we like to take care of our kids and grandbabies."

Anna laughed. "Mama, just let them do something nice for you. Marco would have bought that land himself if he'd thought of it. You don't have to take care of us anymore."

"Like we'll ever stop trying," Grammy mumbled. "What're you going to do with the mill? We weren't too worried about it, just wanted to make sure it didn't fall down or get bull-dozed."

"Well, we *were* going to talk to you two together, but since you're so impatient," Elijah said, rolling his eyes. "We want to renovate it like you all talked about, but we want to do it for Noah. Give him a nice place to live."

"Oh sweetheart, that's a perfect idea," Grammy said. "I'm so glad he's finally home."

"We all are," Anna said.

"While I have you both here, I was thinking of trying to produce apple wine next year. I've made some by hand, and it's yummy, but if I was going to produce it on a larger scale, I'd need the equipment. I have plenty of space to spread out in the basement, but I wanted to check that you all thought it'd be a good idea first."

Anna and Grammy shared a smile. "Of course you can, Eli-baby," Anna said. "Anything you make out of those apples of yours tastes good and sells like hotcakes."

"Um, excuse me?" A woman's voice came from the stairs.

Elijah smiled at Mrs. Weber and waved for her to come in. He stood and offered her his chair. "Hi, Mrs. Weber, what can we do for you?"

Anna and Grammy were quiet. They always went out of their way to avoid talking to her in town and didn't seem to like her much.

"I… I needed to talk to you," she said. She sat down next to Anna. "A little while ago, your boyfriend did a job at my house, and I said some hurtful things. About you."

Elijah wasn't exactly surprised. "I know the town doesn't care much for me, Mrs. Weber. You wouldn't be the first to say hurtful things."

"I know that, but I said them. I spread those words around town for a long time, and that wasn't right."

Grammy's mouth hung open, and Anna's eyes were as wide as saucers.

"Mr. Benson called me out on it. We talked, and, well, it made me think. About a lot of things. I'm truly sorry for the way I've treated you. It may have not been to your face, but the gossip I spread was still cruel. I've wanted to apologize for a while now, but that's not really why I'm here now."

"Thank you, Mrs. Weber, for apologizing. That means a lot," Elijah said, touched. "What did you need?"

"Well, they've been trying to keep quiet about it, but

your parents are in town. They're staying with Delilah Weatherby."

"Those assholes are in town?" Anna growled and jumped up. "I think I'll go say hi."

"Annie sit down," Grammy said. "I don't think Jennifer here is done quite yet."

"Yes, so they've been in town for a week now, and they are saying some horrible things about Elijah around town."

"What are they saying?" Elijah asked softly. He knew his parents were awful, but something inside him kept hoping.

"They said that you are mooching off your grandparents and are unable to provide for your daughter. They said that you are using a crippled man for his money, but you're sleeping around on him. They even said that you kidnapped your deaf brother so you could control his VA benefits."

With each thing she said, Elijah got more and more angry.

"Now, I know all this isn't true, and a lot of people in town know it too, but there are some that are really quick to judge you, like I used to," she said. "I don't know why they're doing this, but I knew you needed to know."

"Thank you, Jennifer," Grammy said. She looked at her daughter. "Do we need to have a gossip war? We know a hell of a lot about them now that Carter's family and his friend Ray did some digging, and we certainly have some truths to hit them with."

"I would be happy to help," Mrs. Weber said. "It

might even be better coming from me, since I used to say bad things about him."

"We might better check with Caden first. He's a sneaky man that lawyer," Elijah said. "He might want us to let them hang themselves."

"Jennifer, can we get back to you?" Grammy patted the woman on her shoulder. "We need to make a battle plan."

"I do want to help," Mrs. Weber said softly. "I want to make amends."

"Thank you, Mrs. Weber," Elijah said. He smiled half-heartedly. "Believe it or not, you taking responsibility for your words and apologizing has made me feel so much better. I keep hoping my parents will be different people, but of course, they can't and won't change. The rest of town though? Maybe there's some hope."

"There's always hope, Eli-baby," Anna said, wrapping him in her warm, familiar embrace.

His phone rang, and it was from one of his colleges. That was odd. Today was the first day of Thanksgiving break. "Hello?"

"Mr. Wilson?" Elijah recognized the voice of the Dean of the School of Business at Ransworth University.

"Hi, Dean Felton. Can I help you with something?"

"Mr. Wilson, I wanted to be the one to tell you, but we aren't going to continue your adjunct contract going forward. Last week, I received some calls about your disturbing lifestyle. First of all, I wasn't aware you were an unwed omega parent, but that is the least of the university's worries. We have an image to uphold, Mr. Wilson, and you certainly don't match it," she said.

Elijah fell into an empty chair, boneless. He shook his head, trying to clear his mind. "Dean Felton, I am going to have to insist that you make a list of everything that was told to you and e-mail it to my lawyer immediately. Did the caller identify him or herself?"

"Lawyers! Now Mr. Wilson, we can terminate your employment at any time. There is nothing illegal in doing that."

"I know, Dean Felton. I am quite aware of the tenuous position of adjunct instructors. However, my lawyer is compiling a harassment and slander case against my parents. Who called you?"

"Um, your father, Steven Wilson. He was very concerned for the university's reputation, Mr. Wilson."

"No, he was very concerned with making my life much harder than it already is, Dean Felton. That, however, is none of your business. Now, you will compose an e-mail listing out the caller's identity and everything he told you. Then you will explain your reasoning in not re-hiring me in the future. Then, you will send it to the e-mail address that I'll text you. If you don't, your university will be hearing from my lawyer in a whole different way. Do you understand, Dean Felton?"

"We won't renew your contract, Mr. Wilson. No matter what any lawyer or court decides."

"Even if you offered me a million dollars, I would never work for you again. If I wasn't concerned about the impact on my current students, I wouldn't finish this term. Now, are you going to write that e-mail or do I need to call my lawyer?"

"Fine," she said. "If it will get rid of you, I'll type it up, notarize it, and fax it to your lawyer. That way I won't be called into court. I can't waste my time on your drama." She hung up the phone.

Elijah immediately called the Dean of the Business Department at Wyndotte County Community College.

"Elijah? Hey, what's going on? I thought for sure you'd be sleeping in and enjoying the first day of Thanksgiving break," Dean Beyer said, voice as chipper as usual.

"Hi Wynonna. Sorry to bother you on break, but have you received any calls about me from my father or mother?"

"Ugh, yes. Your father called me last week and spouted off some nonsense. I don't care if you're a single omega parent. Is this the Victorian period? The rest of it was all garbage. I know you, for goodness sake. I hung up on him and blocked his calls. I meant to e-mail you, but you know how it gets toward the end of the semester."

Elijah laughed, tears filling his eyes. "Yes, I do. If you get time, can you send an e-mail to my lawyer identifying who called and what he said? We're building a harassment and slander case. I know it's a bother, and I am sorry to drag you into my personal business, but the university just fired me because he called them too. I need to nip this in the bud."

"Oh, my God," she said. "I can't believe they fired

you over some phone call. You're one of the best teachers in the department here. I will, of course, send that information right away. Just text me the e-mail account. I can also put in a good word for you at the state college. They were asking about adjuncts, but I knew you were at your limit, so I didn't mention you. Anything you need from me, you let me know, alright Elijah? I'm not kidding. We love you here."

"Thanks, Wynonna. I'll let you know." The call ended, and Elijah turned to see three pairs of wide eyes staring at him.

"They've made their move," Anna said. "It's time we make ours."

CHAPTER 14

Carter finished patching up the steps on Mr. Bartley's porch. How he ended up doing this, he wasn't sure. It wasn't like he could say no to the man. Carter was getting a lot of jobs now, but they were a mix of plumbing and carpentry. He was seriously thinking of begging Juan to move up here and join him in the business.

"Thank you, handsome," Mr. Bartley said, patting at his wet eyes. He had been crying the whole time Carter was there, but he wouldn't tell him a thing. Sad blues music came from the open door. Mr. Bartley was clearly not in a good place. He stood on the porch, dressed in his warm wool leggings and a huge, thick sweater with a colorful trailing scarf.

"You going to finally tell me what's making you cry? I'll do my best to fix it," Carter said.

"Oh, you can't fix this," Mr. Bartley said, sniffling. "I thought Roger and I had something special, but I found out he didn't want to be seen in public with me." His chin wobbled, and he started crying again. "He was even afraid of being seen through my window, didn't want anyone to know he's gay," he said, waving toward the large bay window at the front of the house.

"Well, that guy's an idiot. If I wasn't taken, you and I'd be painting the town," Carter said.

Mr. Bartley giggled, but his tears didn't stop.

Carter put his tools up, then pulled Mr. Bartley into the yard. "Come on, you and I are going to dance. I may not be free to take you out, but I can steal a dance."

"Carter Benson," Mr. Bartley said, laughing, "I would gobble you up if I could."

The two danced in the yard, and neighbors walked by, smiling and waving. Mr. Bartley's tears stopped, and a soft smile played on his lips. He laid his head on Carter's shoulder. After two songs, Mr. Bartley's neighbors on the right, a younger couple in their thirties, came out and joined them, slow dancing to the music. By the sixth song, several other neighbors had joined them in the cold autumn air, dancing and swaying, snow crunching under their feet.

"Can I cut in," an older gruff man asked.

Carter thought he recognized him from the grocery store. Carter looked to Mr. Bartley who nodded shyly. Carter handed him off and watched as the two men danced, whispering and chuckling.

Smiling, he left, heading home early. His phone rang, but he didn't recognize the number so he ignored it. He had gotten two more calls from a woman telling him to stop seeing Elijah or he'd regret it.

The phone rang again, and he grabbed it, fed up. "What?"

"I warned you," the woman said. "I warned you to keep your cripple ass away from Elijah Wilson. You didn't listen, so now you pay. Maybe you ought to check on your house, cripple."

She hung up, leaving him baffled.

What the hell was this woman's problem? Ray had only managed to find out the phone was a burner, making calls from in Hobson Hills, and he'd set up Carter's phone to record every conversation, but that was as far as they could go for now. Carter suspected Elijah's parents were responsible, but knew it would have to be someone working for them.

As he pulled into the driveway, the house looked just fine, but he saw some smoke out on the other side of the orchard. At the trailer. His *old* house. "Shit."

He dialed 911 as he pulled out of the driveway, reported the possible fire, then hung up and raced to the trailer. He hated the thought of the Wilson's property being damaged.

As he parked the van and jumped out, he knew he was too late. The small mobile home was completely engulfed in flames. His main concern became making sure it didn't spread to the apple orchard. The snow on the ground would help, but the trees were bare and dry.

He took a step toward the water hookup, then heard a crunch of feet behind him. He dodged left and grabbed the arm raised above him. He pulled the gun from his assailant's hand and flipped the stranger over his shoulder.

A thick shouldered young man lay on the ground, cradling his arm. Carter looked around, but didn't see anyone else. He flipped the man over on his stomach and pulled his arms behind him, sitting on the man's back. He called 911 again, updated them, then settled in to wait.

"You were supposed to be a cripple. They said it would be easy," the man said, groaning and spitting snow out of his mouth.

"Who's 'they,'" he asked.

"I'm not saying anything, asshole."

"That's a good plan," Carter said and laughed. "You have a charge of arson and assault with a deadly weapon to worry about. Of course, that could be moved up to attempted murder."

"No, man, I wasn't going to kill nobody," the stranger said. "I was just supposed to set the house on fire and scare you real good. That's all."

"That doesn't sound so bad, but still, you're the one here. You're the one who's going to get in trouble."

"Shit, man."

Carter heard sirens, and the police and firetrucks arrived at the same time. An ambulance followed them up the narrow road. The firemen instantly got to work on the house, quickly quenching the flames. Carter recognized Tanner among them.

"Doug Weatherby?" The policeman pulled out his cuffs and quickly secured the young man, reading him his rights. "What the fuck did you do?"

"I was just helping Grandma, Parker. She said this guy needed to be run off. I didn't want to hurt anyone, I swear."

Parker put the man in the back of his car, then came over to talk to Carter. "You have any idea why Delilah Weatherby wants you run off?"

"I've been getting some threatening phone calls, telling me to stay away from Elijah Wilson," he said. He quickly filled the policeman in on the phone calls and Elijah's parents' threats.

"Shit. I've been hearing some rumors around town, and now I've got to wonder if there's a darker purpose to them. Let me make some calls, talk to Doug there, and get back to you."

Carter gave the officer Ray's and Caden's cards, so he could talk to both of them.

The house was gone, burned to the ground. Even knowing it was empty, didn't make Carter feel any better. What if he was living there, and Hotdog had been home?

"Sorry, man," Tanner said, standing beside him. "The house was gone before we got here. At least, it didn't spread to Elijah's trees or the forest on the other side."

"Thanks, Tanner. I'll give Gramps a call and let him know."

He dialed Gramps. Carter had been hesitant to talk to the man, knowing how much Elijah adored his grandfather, but the man was easy to talk to, and they took to one another quickly.

"Hello?"

"Hi, Gramps," he said. "I have some bad news."

After filling him in, Gramps was quiet for a minute. "No one was hurt, right?"

"No, not at all. If I still lived there, Hotdog would be dead, but luckily I don't."

"Come on up to the house. Elijah's got some news, and we'll call that brother of yours. Get his advice too."

"On my way, sir."

Carter quickly drove to Gramps and Grammy's. Elijah, his grandparents, and his aunt and uncles were gathered in the living room. Elijah was pacing the floor, fuming. He ran to Carter when he saw him.

"Are you hurt? I can't believe this happened." He hugged Carter tightly.

"I'm fine, baby. Don't worry," he said. "Now, what news do you have?"

"My parents are in town, staying with Delilah Weatherby, and have been spreading horrible rumors about me."

"Well, that explains why Doug Weatherby's involved."

"They also called the deans at the two schools I worked at, claiming all sorts of nasty things about me."

"What?"

"The dean at the university fired me, but the dean at the community college knows me better and just blocked his calls. They're both sending information to Caden."

"I'm so sorry, baby. Let's talk to Caden and see what he suggests."

"I'm already here, Carter," Caden said from Grammy's phone sitting on the table. "Mr. and Mrs. Wilson have filled me in. The first course of action right now is to pursue the criminal angle we have. I suspect Delilah Weatherby has been the one placing the threatening phone calls on behalf of Elijah's parents. I've already spoken to Officer Jenks, and he is searching her house now. If we can connect them to the crime, we stand a chance of having them actually punished."

"What about the rumors? What should we do?" Marco looked like he wanted to go to town and start knocking heads together.

"As for the rumors, because—unfortunately—Elijah has suffered a financial loss due to them, we have a legal case. I've reviewed both of the deans' information, and we will proceed in suing them for slander and damages. I'm worried about the town gossip though. I suspect they plan on spreading their version of the truth through town, then file for custody of Olive. The local judges would be indirectly influenced."

"So what do you suggest?" Elijah's Uncle Barry asked.

"A battle of words. Choose a well-populated area and simply tell the truth. You said you had an ally? Use her. See if she can rally anyone else. If the town knows the truth, you take away their biggest weapon."

"Talk about an invasion of privacy," Marco mumbled.

"It very much is," Caden agreed. "Elijah should *not*

have to justify himself to a town in order to keep custody of his child. Unfortunately, even in the best of places, there are those who still think poorly of omegas."

"Idiots, the lot of them," Barry said. He himself was an omega, happily at that.

"Agreed," Caden said. "One good point is that Elijah's parents are desperate. Things got hot very fast back in Nevada. The police are still investigating St. Mercy's, but they found enough to start looking closely at the Wilsons. When people get desperate, they make mistakes, and in calling Elijah's schools, they made a big one that can be traced directly to them."

"The Harvest Festival," Grammy said.

"Huh?" Marco asked.

"The Harvest Festival is in two days. All the busy bodies of the town will be there. We rally a gossip army and take them by storm."

"What if my parents are there?" Elijah was pale, unhappy, and worried. Carter cuddled his omega to him.

"Oh, I hope they are," Anna said, smiling. Carter was a little scared of the dainty woman. She loved Elijah like he was her own, and she absolutely hated her brother and his wife.

"Annie," Grammy started.

"No, Mama," Anna said. "We've all kept quiet for far too long. They are the ones who came here. They are the ones who are trying to exploit their own family. I'm done with it."

"She's right, Mama," Marco agreed. "It has gone on long enough."

"It's time to tell the kids," Barry said. "Ernie and Zoe know, but it's time we told them all."

Elijah watched his husband across the breakfast table. He was oh-so-innocently eating his French toast stuffed with lemon ricotta, not a care in the world. Elijah stabbed a bite, maybe a bit too hard, and stuffed it in his mouth.

"You okay, baby?" Carter asked and signed. He smiled at Elijah while reaching over and refilling Olive's orange juice. They all tried to sign when they spoke, to allow Noah to be part of the conversation. Some times were harder than others. Like times when you were really mad.

"Oh, I'm just fine. Perfect. Absolutely perfect."

"Man, I don't think he's feeling perfect," Juan said, looking wary. "What did you do, Carter?" His signing was pretty terrible, but he was trying.

Juan, Ray, and Caden had shown up on their doorstep yesterday morning. Today was the day of the Harvest Festival, and Carter's parents and Cain would be joining them before the festival. Elijah had tried to tell them it wasn't necessary, but they wouldn't hear of it.

"Baby," Carter asked. "Why do you look like you want to stab me?"

Noah slowly reached over and took Elijah's butter knife.

"I love dancing," Elijah said, hissing on the word dance. "Don't you, darling?"

"Yeah, I guess. Don't move as well as I use to, but I still enjoy it."

"You've seen me dance quite a few times. Haven't you, darling?"

"I don't think *darling* is a pet name, Carter," Caden said. "It sounds like a curse."

"I know you like to dance, baby," Carter said with a smile. The fool. "I see you dancing all the time: when you make dinner, feed the animals, get dressed."

"Yet, we have never danced together, have we, husband?"

"No, I guess not," Carter said, looking confused. "Baby, is something wrong?"

"Only that Zoe told me that Liza Berthfield told her that you were dancing with Mr. Bartley," Elijah yelled. "On. His. Lawn."

"Is Mr. Bartley gonna get pregnant now," Olive asked. "'Cause that would be weird."

"No, sweet girl," Juan answered, laughing. "That needs a different kind of dancing, private dancing."

"Okay." She shrugged, then attacked her grapes.

"On. His. Lawn," Elijah repeated. "My husband

won't dance with me, but he'll dance with someone else. On. His. Lawn."

"Baby," Carter started.

"Don't you *baby* me, Carter," he interrupted. "You will dance with me tonight. Every single dance they have at the Festival. Do you hear me?"

"Yes, baby," Carter said, smiling. "I'll dance every single dance with you."

"Are you sure, Papa?" Olive looked worried. "You've seen Daddy dance."

"Olive, eat your breakfast," Elijah said, rolling his eyes. "I dance beautifully."

"You do, baby," Carter said quickly. "I love your dancing."

Juan and Ray snickered, and Caden even managed a smile.

"You three will also dance with me," Elijah decreed. "To give Carter potty breaks. One dance a piece. Got it?"

"Yes, sir," the three men said at once.

Elijah nodded once, firmly, then attacked his breakfast. God, he was starving.

Noah put more bacon on Elijah's plate and refilled his milk. He smiled at his brother. Noah was finally coming out of his shell. He'd been helping Uncle Marco with the cattle and had even taken to spending time with their cousin, Harper, working in his woodshop. It freaked Elijah out a little, knowing that Noah was working with power tools when he couldn't hear, but Harper stayed right with him.

"Juan," Noah said and signed. "Are you moving here to help Carter or not?"

"Yeah, man," Juan said. "My lease is up in January, so I'll move then. Carter is going to start scheduling more jobs for after the New Year."

"Ray," Noah signed. "What about you? Why don't you move here too?"

Ray grinned. The beta was a sweet man and had taken to e-mailing and texting Noah as much as he could. He had told Elijah he wanted the young alpha to have someone of his own to talk to if he needed.

"Yeah. I'll be moving out next week. I only had a month-to-month lease, and Gramps found me a place in town."

"Good," Noah signed, smiling. "I'll go feed the animals."

He stood, and Olive jumped up too. "I want to help, Uncle Noah," she said. "We can play with Billy too." The two took their plates to the sink and walked out the back door.

"He seems to be settling right in," Juan said. "I'm glad. It could have been so much worse, but honestly, to lose something that you rely on so much… I don't know."

"He adapts well," Caden said. "Much better than I thought he would. It helps that he has such a large support system."

"So, when are you moving here, Caden?" Elijah asked, batting his eyes. He decided it was his job to irritate the lawyer, and, to be honest, he would love if Carter's family spent more time there.

Caden raised a brow and ignored Elijah, sipping his coffee. Carter laughed at his brother and snuck a piece of bacon to Hotdog.

Later that morning, Cain, Susan, and John arrived, carrying in their luggage. Elijah had insisted they stay with them, since they had the space. For the first time in over twenty years, the farmhouse's rooms were full. Elijah wasn't sure why that made him so happy, but it did.

Before he knew it, it was close to time for the festival. Elijah was nervous, and he knew exactly why that was. All he had to do was tell the truth, but this town had found him wanting for so long.

Why would it matter to them that he made plenty of money? That he was married now? That he had helped rescue Noah, not kidnapped him? He had learned a long time ago that people would think what they wanted to think.

"Elijah, are you alright?" Susan stepped into his room, looking over all the clothes spread across his bed. "Picking something to wear?"

"Yeah, I can't decide," he said, full of embarrassment. His eyes were filling with tears, and he knew he'd be crying in a minute.

The tears fell, and Susan wrapped him in her arms. "Oh, sweetie," she said. "I know this is hard for you. What's bothering you the most?"

"I love teaching," he said, sobbing. "I'm really good at it. It may not be something I'll ever do full-time, but it was *my* thing."

"Well, you are still teaching at one school, and there

are plenty more to choose from. We'll find you a good one to apply to."

"Not if my reputation is in tatters," he said. "I won't get a reference from the university. I know it."

"You have the other school, and you will have this case to use as evidence. Some schools won't want to deal with that, but some will only care about how well you teach. Those are the schools you want to work for anyway."

"You really think the truth and the lawsuit will make a difference?"

"Sweetie, it will only help so far, but it will make a difference to the people who actually matter. It sounds like Dean Fenton cared about you being a single omega parent, not the nasty lies your father told her. That's not the kind of place you want to work."

"You're right," he said, sniffling. "My head knows you're right, but my heart still hurts. I don't want to see my parents. I don't want to talk to the old, mean gossips. I just want to drink cider, dance with Carter, and play festival games."

"Well, the pregnancy hormones probably aren't helping any either," she said. "You can't help how you feel but know that you don't have to do a single thing. Today, we'll fight for you, alright? Today, we'll carry this burden for you. You've had to deal with town gossip for a long time, and I know a person gets used to it after a while, but that doesn't make it any less hurtful. We'll deal with it, sweetie. You worry about that pie you're entering into the contest. I know Cain and Juan were both thinking about taking a bite out of it."

"What? They better not touch my pie," Elijah said. He grabbed a pair of loose-waisted, tight-legged jeans and a large cream colored sweater. "Go guard my pie. I'll hurry up and get dressed."

AT THE DOOR, Elijah inspected his army. Susan carried a whole pie and wore a warm designer coat, leggings, and a bright red knitted scarf and hat. Ernie had been at it again.

All the men, except Cain, wore warm coats and their own Ernie scarves. Cain's coat wasn't at all practical for the cold Main weather.

Olive held her Uncle Noah's hand, dressed warmly and wearing a little knitted hat shaped like an owl. Even Hotdog and Winston were coming, dressed in their own knitted sweaters.

"Cain, you can't wear that coat. What were you thinking? It's thirty-three degrees outside. Carter, grab one of Gramps' old coats out of the closet please," Elijah ordered.

His Georgia boys were a little hard-headed. "Juan, I love your Mohawk, I do, but you really should wear a hat. Carter, will you grab my plaid earflap hat? The one Ernie gave me last week? That'll match his coat."

Once everyone was properly attired, they piled into their cars and drove to the festival. Cars lined the streets and filled the parking lots. Hobson Hills went all out for the Fall Festival, and Elijah planned on having some fun.

His cousins waited for him at the entrance, all ten of them, from the youngest, thirteen-year-old Hannah, to the eldest, twenty-four-year-old Zoe. All of them wore the same expression: angry and fierce.

Zoe stepped forward. "My dads, Uncle Marco, Uncle Benett, and Gramps are already in the festival. We have our game plan ready, but Elijah, all you need to worry about is having fun." She gestured to the youngest cousins. "Carter, you, Olive, and Elijah will go with Hannah, Milly, and Allison. You will dance. You will play games. You will drink apple cider. Do I make myself clear?"

Elijah looked at Susan.

She smiled and shrugged. "I may have made a phone call."

He rolled his eyes, but honestly, it felt good to not have to worry about this. His family would take care of it.

"Juan, Ray, and Caden, you will go with Harper to the dunking booth. When you see the horror couple, you will serve them their papers. Make sure to be loud and dramatic," Zoe continued.

Juan smiled and rubbed his hands together. "I love drama!"

"Mr. and Mrs. Benson, you'll go with Ernie, Abel, and Uncle Matt, Aunt Anna's husband. You all will meet up with Mrs. Weber and her cronies. For once, that group is working with us. You will begin to spread the news of Elijah's wedding and, of course, how happy you are with your new son-in-law."

"I can toss in how he has already increased Carter's trust fund. Our accountant loves him," John said, smiling. Elijah had a feeling Juan wasn't the only one who liked drama.

"Good idea," Zoe said. "Gramps and his group are already spreading the word on Elijah's skills in investing." She glared at Elijah. "Really, Eli, you could have told us that you invested money for our parents. I don't think any of us knew we had trust funds. I, for one, had no idea I was worth so much money."

"Seriously, Elijah," Hannah said. "I already make more monthly than most of my friends' parents. I am so going to veterinary school, and I'm not going to worry about the cost. I'm just going to be what I want to be. Do you know how freeing that is?"

"That was the plan, Hanny," he said, smiling. He wanted his family to be able to pursue whatever career they wanted, without worrying about money. They had so much to offer the world, and nothing was going to hold them back.

"I may have a lot too, but I'm still going to be a mechanic," Shawn said. "Cars are my happy place."

Zoe laughed and hugged the young beta. "Town could use a good mechanic, so hurry up with it," she said. "Anyway, Cain and Noah, you will come with me. It's time to set things straight about Noah's situation. Cain, I want you to casually mention the investigation going on back in Nevada."

Cain nodded, looking a little silly in Gramps' big, old coat.

"Shawn, Janelle, and Evan, you all will scatter and talk. Share Elijah's news with the world!"

"Where's Grammy and Aunt Anna," Elijah asked.

Zoe grimaced. "Grammy is trying to keep Aunt Anna from murdering your parents in public, so you'll see them around, but their job is merely to not cause violence."

Milly and her younger sister, Allison, shared a look and grinned.

"I kinda want to see Mom get in a fight," Allison said. "I've never seen her so mad before, and trust me, I've made her plenty mad."

"Seriously," Evan said. "She's even madder than she was at that one university when they rejected my application and said an omega couldn't get into medical school. I thought she was going to burn the place to the ground."

Elijah would have helped her do it too. Evan had a 4.0 GPA, and he was easily the best candidate that applied. Well, Elijah could possibly be biased, but he really thought Evan was the best. Luckily, another school was more than happy to take him.

"Okay, everyone clear on their role?" Zoe stood in front of the group like an avenging angel leading her army to battle.

"Sir, yes, sir," everyone shouted.

CHAPTER 16

Carter watched his mate giggle as he hugged the massive stuffed llama to his chest. He'd spent a good hour winning stuffed animals for his husband, daughter, and three teenaged cousins. All five hugged their prizes and laughed as they swayed on the hay ride.

The autumn air was cold and crisp, but the scenery more than made up for it. They wound through the woods surrounding the town, colorful leaves covering the ground. Bare maple and oak trees mixed with green pines. Pumpkins and hay bales decorated the path, adding to the natural scenery. Steaming cups of apple cider were handed out, and the smell of cinnamon and apples filled the air.

Carter wrapped an arm around his omega, cuddling him close on their bale of hay. Hotdog sat in his lap, happy to be out and about. Olive and Winston sat across from them, in the middle of her older cousins, laughing and happy.

Carter couldn't keep the smile from his face. In the back of his mind, he worried about how things were progressing, but here, he couldn't resist his omega's smile.

Josh and Cassidy Weber sat on the other side of the girls, and Carter didn't like the looks Josh kept exchanging with Milly. Damn teenage boys. The two had insisted on helping their mother when she told them what she had planned. It still surprised him to see the change in the woman. She really was a nice person, just human. He was proud of her for taking responsibility and changing.

"What's next, Papa?" Olive hugged her unicorn to her and watched him with adoring eyes. He couldn't believe how much these two loved him. Him!

A quickly drawn breath grabbed his attention. The woman seated next to them watched, mouth hanging open.

"Are you hungry, sweetheart?" he asked Olive, ignoring the woman. "I think your Daddy's belly just growled, or there's a bear out there."

Elijah snorted and smacked his arm. "I could eat."

"Then he should eat," Olive said. "Shelly says that when someone's having a baby, Santa thinks they should eat and drink a lot."

Carter thought the stranger's eyes were going to fall out of her face. "Baby, you hear that? Santa says you get to eat and drink anything you want," he said, grinning smugly. His omega carried his baby. Yeah, they were all his.

"Good, because I want Shepard's pie, clam chowder,

and funnel cake," Elijah said. "As soon as possible, please," he added politely.

"There you go, Olive," Carter said. "Food's our next stop."

"Then dancing," Allison asked. "Carter's going to dance with you until the pie contest, right Elijah?"

Elijah grinned. "Yes, he is."

They unloaded from the hay ride when it finished and watched Elijah eat for over an hour. Finally, he was full, and the girls watched Olive and the dogs while he danced with his omega.

Elijah shook his butt, waved him arms, and giggled through six songs. Carter stood with him, swaying back and forth, and just watched his mate be happy.

On the seventh song, someone tapped his shoulder. Mr. Bartley stood behind him.

"May I cut in handsome? Your omega has some moves."

Carter grinned and watched Elijah size up the older man. Mr. Bartley wore high-heeled boots, black leggings, and a large, colorful designer sweater. His make-up was flawless.

"Bring it on, Mr. Bartley. Let's see what you got," Elijah said.

Carter left them to it and made a bathroom run. When he came out, he stopped to check his messages, overhearing a group of adults talking.

"I can't believe his parents are trying to take his daughter away," a woman said. "She was in my kindergarten class, and I know for a fact that she's well cared for and happy."

"Well, he's a single omega. It's a logical assumption," a man said.

Another woman smacked his arm, hard. "Don't be stupid, Carl. Do you honestly think your omega dad couldn't have raised you on his own if he had to?"

"Of course he could have, but he's different," Carl said.

"Why?"

"I don't know. He just is."

"It's because you know him, so you know he's as capable as any alpha or beta. You don't know Elijah Wilson though. Trust me, he is a good man. You remember when the Randel family attended the Winter Festival out at Farm Fresh, and everyone was really surprised?"

"Yeah, that was weird, because he had just been laid off, so he shouldn't have been spending money on that kind of thing. It takes a good fifty bucks to get a family his size in there," Carl said.

"Okay, well, first, don't judge other people's financial situations, honey. Second, they had a *mystery* friend give them those tickets. Martha told me they were in her mailbox with a sweet note of encouragement. Deacon and her became obsessed with finding out who it was, because I think he left more than tickets in that mailbox. Anyway, she found out it was Elijah Wilson. Does that sound like someone who would kidnap his brother so he could steal his VA benefits?"

"No," Carl laughed. "I knew that wasn't true though.

Saw Noah out working with Marco's cattle. He looked as happy as a clam."

"My point, honey, is that Steven and Rachael Wilson are liars," Carl's wife said.

"That is the truth," the first woman said. "I remember Steven in school. He could charm the pants off any girl he talked to. He'd get what he wanted, then treat them like garbage afterward. His brothers and sister would get so mad at him."

"Debbie, you would know. Didn't you date him in high school?" a different woman said. "They made a good point about his finances though. If he can't afford to take care of his child, then she needs someone who can."

"Oh, my God, Rhonda," Carl's wife said. "Like his huge family wouldn't help him out in any way, and if Olive did need to be taken in by a relative, it sure as shit wouldn't be those two. This is the third time they've been in town since Elijah was born. I asked my mom to make sure. They didn't even want to see their own child."

"She doesn't need to go to anyone else," Debbie said. "I'm telling you, when she was in my class, there wasn't a single sign that she suffered in anyway. Hell, she brought snacks every day for two students who couldn't afford their own. They got free lunches, but a kid needs more than that in a day. She kept them fed, and Shelly Pettit's her best friend now. That's not a child who goes hungry."

"Didn't you guys hear though," the last member of their group asked. "Apparently, he's loaded. I knew he had an MBA, but I think everyone assumed he didn't use it. His father-in-law said that he handles investments for the whole Wilson family. Plus, Jennifer Wilson and her friends all said that Steven and Rachel were lying out their asses about Elijah."

Carter grinned, hearing enough and turned the corner. Maybe this whole *battle of words* idea hadn't been so bad.

Then again, maybe that was too hasty.

When he got back to his group, Elijah was rocking a crying Olive in his arms, and Mr. Bartley and Elijah's cousins were standing in front of them protectively. Rachel and Steven Wilson were yelling at their son, and a crowd had gathered around them.

"You're suing us? How dare you! We're your parents, and you're suing us for telling the truth to this shitty little town," Rachel screamed.

"It's all your fault, you stupid omega," Steven added. "All you had to do was give us a little money. That's all you had to do, but no, you steal our son and refuse to give us what we deserve. We'd have money if you hadn't stolen your brother from us."

"You two need to shut up," Allison yelled back. "All you do is spread lies."

"You threatened to sue for custody of Olive if Grammy and Gramps didn't give you money," Milly said angrily. "Then you dare to act like victims."

"You two are disgusting bullies," Hannah added. "Elijah's the best dad in the world. Well, other than mine. He loves Olive, takes good care of her, and takes good care of the whole family. What do you do? Try to steal money from your *family*? Lock your son up in a psych ward? Blackmail your other son? You're garbage."

"You even made Elijah lose one of his jobs," Allison said. "You called and spread your lies at his workplace. I may only be fourteen, but even I know that's low."

The two adults started backing away, but the people surrounding the scene didn't move. Elijah stood, holding Olive's hand.

"Don't think we don't know that you talked Delilah Weatherby into threatening my husband. She got her grandson to burn Carter's former house down and threaten him with a gun. We know you're behind that and the police do too. I would worry about that more than my lawsuit."

"Husband? That cripple's not your husband," Rachel screeched.

"Oh, yes, I am," Carter said, standing beside his omega. "Elijah was just fine on his own. He doesn't need me, but I lucked out because Olive and him want me. We've been married for over a month. Maybe if your heads weren't stuck so far up your asses, you would have known that."

"How could anyone want some filthy, used omega," Rachel asked, voice rising.

"Don't you dare talk about him like that." Aunt Anna pushed her way through the crowd. Uh oh. Things could get ugly.

"He's my son," Rachel yelled. "I'll talk about him any way I want to."

"Your son?" Anne said, incredulous. "Your son?"

"Yes, mine, you stupid bitch."

"Your son? *We* changed his diapers when he was a baby. *We* fed and clothed him. *We* were the ones who dried his tears when he asked why his mommy and daddy didn't love him. I'm the one who rocked him to sleep, sang him lullabies.

"Marco taught him how to fish and gave him his first pet—a hamster named Ham and Eggs the Third," she continued. "He taught him how to love and take care of animals. Barry went school shopping with him at the start of every year, taught him to dance, helped him apply to colleges. After that asshole left him pregnant, Marco is the one that talked him into finishing school, then coming home."

The Bensons and the rest of the Wilsons stood with the crowd, watching Anna. Juan and Ray stood behind Carter and Elijah, keeping the crowds back.

"Mama taught him how to cook and keep a home, how to take care and love everyone. Daddy taught him how to raise apple trees and how to tap the best maple trees for syrup. He taught him how to be patient and thankful for everything the world gives him."

Grammy stood next to Gramps, tears streaming down her face. Gramps arms wrapped around his wife, and the hard look in his eyes made Carter feel a little sorry for Steven and Rachel Wilson. Just a little.

"We all are the ones who love him. I didn't carry him, but he's *my* son. He's Marco and Barry's son. He's Mama and Daddy's son." She stood in front of her brother, ignoring his fuming wife. "He is nothing to you, Steven. He is nothing to *that* woman. You gave up that right when you left him with Mama when he was literally one week old. I heard you that night. You said you wouldn't raise an omega. That they were useless. That Barry, your own damn brother, was useless. Eli-baby became mine that night. He's *mine*. His daughter is mine. Now, Noah's mine too." The tiny blond looked straight into the large alpha's eyes, standing on her tiptoes. "You do not want to fuck with me and mine, Steven. Take your whore and get the fuck out of here."

"We'll see you in court, you stupid bitch," Rachel screamed as Steven dragged her away. The two tried to disappear into the crowd.

"Steven and Rachel Wilson?" Parker and two other police officers surrounded the couple. "You are under arrest for assault and arson."

"What the fuck are you talking about, you pathetic, limp-dicked, asshole?" Rachel screamed.

"You must be mistaken, officer," Steven said, trying to remain calm.

Parker read them their rights and the officers hauled off a screaming Rachel and a shocked Steven.

"Drama," Mr. Bartley said in awe. "So much drama."

"Oh, my God, Mom," Allison said in the silence. "I've never loved you more."

"It would have been nice if you smacked Rachel a few times though," Milly added. "Before they got arrested."

Elijah jumped into his aunt's arms. "Thank you, Aunt Anna. Thank you for saying all of that, even though you didn't have to. The girls were handling things."

"Rachel grabbed Olive's arm," Mr. Bartley said. "She was trying to drag her away while Steven was yelling at Elijah. Little Allison here stomped on Rachel's toe and punched her in the stomach. Milly and Hannah grabbed Olive and got her back to Elijah before anyone else even noticed Rachel had grabbed her."

"Good girls," Grammy said, hugging her granddaughters.

"What did I miss?" Mrs. Weber and her two friends pushed through the dispersing crowd. "Do you need anything, Elijah? Cassidy, Josh, what's going on?"

Elijah just smiled and shook his head. He and Anna took an upset Olive to get some more funnel cake.

"Just Aunt Anna and the police taking care of business, Mrs. Weber," Carter said. "Thank you for helping out tonight. We appreciate what you and your friends did. I know Elijah's parents would be hard pressed right now to succeed if they tried to sue for custody of Olive."

She smiled. "I know the town is more informed too. We can't change everyone's minds, but quite a few people will think a little harder before they listen to rumors."

Carter's parents took Winston and Hotdog's leashes and picked up Elijah and Olive's stuffed animals from where they sat on a bench. "We'll go on and get home, son," John said. "Josh there recorded the whole incident, so we'll make sure to collect it and add it to our evidence."

"Take care, darling," his mother said, kissing his

cheek. "Your omega's going to crash from his high tonight. Make sure you're there for him."

The rest of their group took off, leaving Noah, Gramps, Grammy, Barry, and Marco at their table. When Elijah, Anna, and Olive came back with their sugary treats, they sat and talked, laughing and enjoying the late afternoon. They watched the pie contest, Elijah winning third place.

They made plans for Thanksgiving and talked about renovating the old mill. Through hugs, smiles, and claps on the back, they each told Elijah, Noah, and Olive how much they were loved.

CHAPTER 17

Elijah looked around the packed dining table. All the Wilsons and the Bensons were present, as were Juan and Ray. Evan had brought a few buddies from college that didn't have families to go home to for the holiday, and Olive had invited her best friend Shelly's family. Grammy's barn was full, and Thanksgiving was in full swing.

Elijah sat on his alpha's lap and ate his second serving, already planning on a third. His hunger seemed constant.

"There's a nice cabin on the lake, John, that's up for sale," Gramps said. "It'd make a nice vacation home, and give you all another reason to come visit more often."

"We'll have to go take a look at it while we're here," Carter's father said.

"Oh, darling, this cranberry sauce is simply amazing," Susan told Grammy. "Please tell me you'll

141

share your recipe." The two women laughed and compared stories of previous family dinners.

The rest of their family and friends mixed together, talking and signing. Olive ran around the room with Shelly and Shelly's older brother and younger sister. The kids' table would be getting bigger soon enough.

Noah sat with Harper and Ray, talking and seeming to be enjoying the food. His brother was considering getting some horses. Noah loved them and working with them gave him some much needed peace. Uncle Marco was trying to convince him to use the acreage that came with the old mill to build a barn and buy some horses. They'd see what Noah decided.

Cain sat with Evan and his friends. They talked about school and dealing with difficult professors. Caden and Juan, surprisingly, sat with the teenagers. They hadn't buried their head in their pie yet, so that must have been going well.

Zoe sat next to him and Carter, Janelle on the other side, and Ernie and Abel across from them.

"I think Harper's in love with this guy he met online," Zoe said.

"What? Do tell," Abel said, grinning slyly.

"He's a graphic designer, and Harper hired him for his furniture website. Once the job was done, though, they kept talking. Now he video chats with him every night."

"Oh, my God, that is so sweet," Abel said.

"His dad told him to go to Florida and get his omega. He said to just toss him over his shoulder and bring him home, so the family can love on him. Apparently, he doesn't have any family."

"That is called kidnapping," Carter said, looking at Elijah.

Elijah's cheeks were stuffed full of mash potatoes, and he listened avidly to his cousins' conversation. His alpha wrapped his arms around him, resting his head on top of Elijah's.

Family was pretty great.

~

Two months later

ELIJAH ARCHED UP, pressing into Carter's mouth. His alpha's mouth caressed his rounded belly, pressing small kisses into his skin. The two men lay naked, spread out on their bed.

Elijah's dick was hard, aching, and his hole was slick and stretched already, waiting to be filled by his alpha. He moaned as Carter finally took his dick in his mouth, sucking him deeply. His hands cupped his husband's head, his legs spreading wide.

A few minutes of Carter's tongue and mouth were more than enough to have Elijah coming. Carter swallowed his cum, every drop, and slowly kissed his way up to Elijah's mouth. Elijah could taste himself on his husband's lips.

"You taste so good, baby," Carter whispered.

Elijah kissed him again, wrapping his legs around

his alpha's waist. "Come inside me, alpha-mine," he said. "I need you."

He didn't have to ask twice. A few moments later, and Carter was pounding into him, filling him. Elijah felt his arousal growing again, growing and growing, almost there. In seconds, he was coming for a second time, his channel squeezing his alpha's cock tightly.

Carter grunted, pouring cum into him. They lay in bed, tangled together, sweaty, and happy.

"Love you, baby," Carter said.

"Love you too, alpha-mine." He listened to Carter's heartbeat as he drew closer to sleep. "Is it bad that I don't feel happy about what happened today? That I don't really feel anything for my parents now?"

Elijah wanted to feel happy, or angry, or anything really, but when he thought of his parents, he felt absolutely nothing.

"I don't think so, baby. You've been let down by them for so long, maybe you've gotten numb to it. I do know that they can't bother you anymore."

Elijah's parents owed him a hefty amount of money and had a restraining order keeping them from both him and Olive. They were also in jail for six more months. That wasn't considering time they'd likely serve for what they had done to Noah. Nevada had their own case against the couple, and it was progressing well for Noah. Not so well for their parents.

"I'm not happy or mad. I'm just glad it's over. Glad I don't ever have to see them again," Elijah said. "I have my family. I have you and Olive. I can't think of anything better."

"Me neither, baby. Me neither. Well, maybe a hamster."

"No, Carter! You are not to adopt anymore animals from Doctor Grover."

"But he doesn't have anywhere to go. We could name him Ham and Eggs the Fourth."

"For the love of apples, Carter!"

~

Three months later

OLIVE WAS PLAYING with Hotdog and Winston in front of the fireplace on the living room floor. Hotdog had grown in the past few months. He required constant grooming for his long, shaggy hair, but Elijah couldn't find it in himself to mind. Carter loved that dog so much.

Susan and John would be coming by to pick up Olive for the weekend in about an hour. The two had bought the cabin on the lake as a vacation home. They had already come up twice since Thanksgiving. Elijah thought it wouldn't be long until they retired there.

Cain and Caden seemed happy to stay in Georgia, but each of them video chatted with their niece once a week. They also sent her books all the time. She already had two bookcases full and loved to read them. Elijah and Olive were plotting how to get Carter's brothers to Maine.

Elijah watched Hodges sleep in his bed on the living room table. Olive had insisted that the little critter really wanted to come play in the living room. The hedgehog really wanted to sleep. Ham and Eggs the Fourth slept in his soft, hamster-shaped bed house as well. Boo curled up against Elijah's side, purring and sleeping. Lazy animals.

Elijah heard Carter pull up outside. He pushed himself off the couch, ignoring Boo's disgruntled hiss, and waddled to the door. He was six months pregnant, and he waddled. There was no other way to describe it. The doctor said that having twins would mean he got bigger faster than if he was having a single. All Elijah got from that was that he was really fat and it was okay.

Carter poked his head in the door and gave him a nervous smile. *What does he have to be nervous about,* Elijah wondered. Wait. His last job of the day was at the veterinarian's clinic.

"Damn it, Carter," Elijah said softly, shooting Olive a look. "What did you adopt this time?"

"Uh, just come look."

"Carter!"

"Please?"

Like he could resist his alpha. Elijah sighed and waddled to the door. Carter kissed him gently and held his hand as they left the porch. Carter's van was pulling a horse trailer.

"Doc said that they can't be separated because they love each other, just like us. When they were adopted out before, it was to two separate homes and both of them wouldn't eat or drink anything. When they were back together again, they were fine."

Elijah looked into the trailer. He came face to face with a cow, a long-haired Scottish cow to be exact. Next to the shaggy, red giant was a white and grey llama with a flower tucked in its harness.

"Their names are Wayne and Garth," Carter said. "Can we keep them?"

The Blue Solace Series – science fiction/fantasy, gay romance, mpreg

1. The Mercenary's Mate – https://amzn.to/2MAOFEH
2. The General's Mate – https://amzn.to/2G1abRE
3. The Soldier's Mate – https://amzn.to/2S7R6ng
4. The Lieutenant's Mate – https://amzn.to/2THZ47w
5. The Engineer's Mate – https://amzn.to/2HpI4vH
6. The Captain's Mate – https://amzn.to/2knP03W

The Hobson Hills Omegas – non-shifter, gay romance, mpreg, omegaverse

1. Falling for the Omega – https://amzn.to/2BgWURV
2. Snow Kisses for My Omega – https://amzn.to/2TdDiol
3. Romancing the Omega – https://amzn.to/2UNENKD
4. Healing the Omega – https://

amzn.to/2FNcXrY

5. A Pint for my Omega – https://
   amzn.to/2XItQf7
6. Unraveling the Omega – https://
   amzn.to/2xRCnRL
7. The Alpha's Christmas Wish – *Coming
   December 2019*

Hobson Hills Shorts – short stories from the world of
Hobson Hills Omegas

1. The Beta's Love Song – https://
   amzn.to/2UrRPNN
2. Bennett's Dream – https://
   amzn.to/2GwSpG3
3. Justin's Journey – https://amzn.to/2DhW1t1

The Silver Isles – paranormal, merman, gay romance,
mpreg, paranormal

1. The Guppy Prince – *Coming Soon*
2. The Not so Little Merman – *Coming Soon*
3. The Sea Witch – *Coming Soon*

If you would like to keep up with releases, please like and
follow me on Facebook at @cwgrayauthor, visit my website
at https://cwgray-author.com, or join C.W. Gray's Reading
Nook on Facebook.

Unedited excerpt from *Snow Kisses for My Omega* –
Book Two in The Hobson Hills Omegas

"Wow, that's just beautiful, Gray," Harper Wilson said,
looking at the baby book I mailed him a few days ago.
The handsome alpha grinned, the gap between his
front teeth absolutely charming. "I don't know why
you won't try to publish this. I'm lending it to my
cousin, just so you know. He just announced he was
pregnant right before Thanksgiving."

"Ah, that's great," Grayson Bishop said, glad the
screen only ever showed him from the neck up. His big
pregnant belly would have given him away a long time
ago. "I remember you said he got married just a few
weeks before then. Are they happy about the baby,
since it happened so quickly?" He didn't know why he
cared, but he wanted to hear about some alpha actually
caring about their baby.

"Oh yeah." Harper said. "Carter is ecstatic." Of course he was, Gray thought. Maybe he was the only one that ended up with an alpha boyfriend who didn't want kids. The asshole had dumped him seconds after Gray showed him the pregnancy test.

"I wish you could have made it for Thanksgiving. When are you going to visit, Gray," Harper asked, eyes watching his face closely. "You said you wanted to get out of Florida. Of course it's really cold right now, but the snow's beautiful. You'd like it and I have plenty of space."

If he had met Harper seven months ago, Gray would already be moved to Maine. He was absolutely crazy about the woodworker. He was kind, gentle, intelligent, so damn hot, the whole package. No, instead of meeting Harper, he met Ted. Now, Harper wouldn't talk to him if he knew Gray was six months pregnant with another alpha's child.

"Maybe... maybe in few months," he said, putting the handsome alpha off again. In a few months, he'd be having a baby. He'd have to come clean to Harper, and then he'd lose him.

"Hey fatty!" His roommate's voice called from outside his door.

"Shit, I have to go, Harper, talk to you later."

"But, Gray..."

Gray hurriedly closed the video call and jumped out of his seat. Dorian forced open the door, popping the lock. Again.

"I'm not fat, Dorian. I'm pregnant."

"That baby ain't sitting in your ass, Fatty," he said. "You need to pack your shit and get out by the end of the week."

"What? I have this room for another three months."

"Landlord don't want a whore omega on his property. You're lucky I talked him into a week. He wanted you out tonight."

Tears welled in his eyes. "I'm not a whore. I've only even slept with two guys my whole life. I'm pregnant. It happens all the time."

"Don't care, Fatty. Just make sure your shit's out by Friday." Dorian left, letting the door bang shut behind him.

Gray sat on the bed and let himself cry. He wiped his face and cupped his belly. "It's okay baby. I'll take care of us, okay. It might get hard, but I'm here for you and I love you."

He wiped his nose on his sleeve and spied the bag of tacos he left on his desk for dinner. He always ate dinner after talking with Harper. His appetite was always really good after seeing the handsome alpha. He made him feel safe and special.

"Come on baby, let's sing the taco song and have dinner." He grabbed the bag and set it on the bed.

"Taco, taco, taco," he sang to his belly. "This baby loves tacos. They're so yummy, so let's stuff them in my tummy."

He devoured the tacos, all four of them, then sat down again. He had to think about packing all his things. He had tons of books and his collection of Pop figures. "At least I didn't go and adopt a dog like I wanted," he mumbled. "I can't even take care of myself and you baby boy."

He lay down for the night, not noticing his laptop open, video call still streaming.

Unedited excerpt from *The Mercenary's Mate* – Book
One in the Blue Solace Series

Silverlight System, Planet Vextonar

"Next up is a real gem, gentle folks!" The auctioneer
leered toward the large crowd at the bottom of the
stage. He was a Betonize-human hybrid, sharp teeth a
glaring white. "This little girl's part Prime and part
Lower. Don't see that on Vextonar too often."

The crowd's boisterous laughter and cheering filled
the room. Eight people had already been auctioned off,
and the day was still young. Leti Ando gritted his teeth
and awkwardly shuffled his feet. The bulky cast on his
lower leg made him slower than normal, and there
were too many strangers here, too much movement.
He wanted to be in his rooms, reading the new Old-
Earth journal he'd gotten his hands on.

Draif shot him a sympathetic look. Leti's best friend

was no less uncomfortable in the auction house but had insisted on coming with him. "You knew it'd be like this, Master," Draif whispered.

Leti glared at his friend, his black eye and busted lip protesting the expression. "I hate it when you call me that."

Draif gave him a small smile, dark eyes on the stage. "I know. Why do you think I do it?" His smile faded. "It's her, Leti."

Leti startled, stumbling and knocking into some of the men around him. He did his best to ignore the grumbles, his heart beating fast in his chest. Monty slipped from his head to his shoulder, and Draif grabbed his arm to steady him. For such a small, slender man, Draif had a strong and sure grip that came in handy when Leti's clumsiness attacked.

Leti ignored the grumbles around him, eyes locked on the stage. A modestly dressed woman stood tall. She held a whimpering, blanket-wrapped bundle in her arms.

"This little lady is up for sale," the Auctioneer said. "She comes from a Prime daddy and his mistress, a Lower woman. Unnamed infant, but good potential. Mommy's dead and Daddy don't want a Lower brat, so there won't be no contest of ownership once she's bought. We'll start bidding at 250? Can I get 250?"

Leti sighed and closed his eyes. "I can't believe Father is selling his own child. I hate that he deals in slavery at all, but his own daughter?"

"Yeah, well, he didn't seem to like your opinion too much last night when you brought it up." Draif grabbed his hand and squeezed. "Not that he needs much excuse to beat the shit out of you. It was the threat to sell you too that worries me the most."

It wasn't appropriate for a bed-slave to hold his master's hand, but the two of them had never been *appropriate*. Nothing was normal about a Prime citizen who didn't have sex with his bed-slave, little less treat him like a slave, and nothing was normal about a bed-slave who was demisexual and had a scarred face and damn good fighting skills.

Draif had been Leti's best friend since they were both fifteen. Leti's father gave him to his son and told him to dominate the "broken" slave and prove himself a man. The arrogant Prime often told his son that he was so fat and awkward that no one would ever want him, especially with his attention always on his studies and research.

Leti might be a breeder male, able to have children, but his father assured him no one would ever offer for him like they would a daughter. And love? According to his father, no one could ever love him, not even some mixed breed alien. Being a breeder male showed his blood was too diluted to be human enough. There was too much Wello blood in his ancestry. Father always blamed Leti's mother for it, but never to her face. He was an arrogant bully, not stupid.

In his father's mind, a bed-slave would guarantee that Leti would at least be a man in the bedroom. Leti tried not to complain too much, though. Draif had proven to be the best thing that ever happened to him. He was his loyal confidant and best friend from the start and soon became his assistant, body guard, and overall jack-of-all-trades.

Where Leti struggled in anything outside of his books and pets, Draif could seemingly master any skill if he set his mind to it. More importantly, though, Leti loved Draif more than anything in all the galaxies. He was his brother in all but blood. His family.

"620 to the Drall in the corner. Can I get 630, anyone? 630?"

"Is your lawyer bidding?" Draif whispered.

Leti looked at his communicator. "Yes. He'll keep topping whatever's offered. She'll be ours in a few minutes."

"You father won't like that, Leti. What are we going to do? We can't hide her in your rooms until she's eighteen. I guess we could put her in Wobble's stable, but who wants to live with an Old-Earth Llama?" Draif paused and eyed his friend. "Well, except for you."

Leti grinned. "When I get her, you are going to take her to the spaceport. Talk with Dottie. She's going to sneak all of us on a random ship going out of the system. Father would be alerted if we used our passports, so we have to sneak, at least at first. Once we're out of the Silverlight system, I can tear up your contract as well as hers. You'll both be free."

Draif squeezed his hand tight. His eyes left the stage, widened in disbelief. "We're leaving the system?"

Leti snorted. "I've given you several chances to leave over the last ten years, but you wouldn't go."

"I couldn't possibly leave you behind. I love you," he said with no hesitancy. "What about your menagerie?"

Draif looked at the vexal newt happily perched on Leti's shoulder. "Monty here wouldn't be a problem, but you can't possibly expect to sneak all of them onboard a ship and I know you won't leave them." Draif shook his head, dumbfounded. "What about money? How will you survive? I can easily get work, but you're a trained historian. They aren't exactly rolling in credits." He paused, already forming a plan. "I could work and you could stay home and take care of the baby. You'd be good at that. You love. It's your thing, and in the end, that's all it really takes. We can figure out how to feed her and change a diaper."

"1050! Can I get 1100? Anyone? 1100?"

"Dottie assures me it will be fine. She's picked out a Drellian cargo vessel and my pets are heading there as we speak, even Wobble." Leti checked his comm, then continued, "As for money, I've been saving for a long time. Do you really think I spend all the credits Father gives me monthly?"

"He's always complaining that you drain his pocket, but I thought he was just being cheap. All you buy are books on your tablet, presents for me, and things for the pets. I think the most expensive thing you bought was the tablet. It came from the Anchor's Rest System, right? Our system is seriously behind on tech."

Leti nodded. "I don't usually use more than a quarter of the allowance. I've been saving my pay from my publications too. It's certainly not much, but I didn't become a historian to make money. I never thought I'd have to." Leti laughed ruefully. "I'm a privileged Prime, right?"

Draif let go of his hand and smacked his arm. "No self-deprecation allowed! We are who we are, there's no changing that. Especially on this world. It's not like you can change castes and become a Worker. Anyways, the gods know that no one deserves to be related to your father or psycho mother." He smiled sadly and nodded toward Leti's broken ankle. "Their love hurts."

Draif looked worried. "Are you going to pack and bring my things too?"

"Of course! Melinda has already started packing for us."

"Will she alert your father?"

Leti checked his comm again. Things were on track. "No. She's the one who urged me to start saving credits when I was twelve. Once we leave, she's going to go to Rothwell and work with her daughter."

"Good." Draif's couldn't seem to stop smiling. "We're really doing this?"

"1520 to the gentleman at the front! 1600 anyone? 1600? Going once. Going twice. Sold to the gentleman in the blue coat!"

Despite his worry, Leti grinned. "Yes. We're really doing this."

Buy Here: My Book